The Romans discover Britain

Front cover: A mosaic from North Africa, showing the ocean portrayed as a god. In Greek mythology Oceanus was the son of Uranus, the sky god, and the goddess of the earth. He was married to Tethys. As all other rivers were seen to be linked to the ocean, the god Oceanus was thought to be the father of all river gods.

CAMBRIDGE SCHOOL CLASSICS PROJECT
CLASSICAL STUDIES 13-16

Book I. The Romans discover Britain

compiled by MIKE HUGHES and MARTIN FORREST

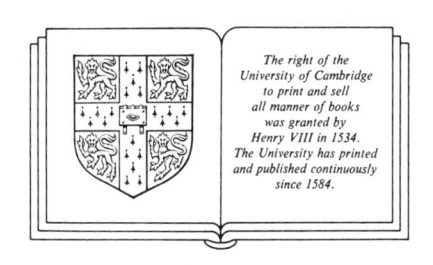

*The right of the
University of Cambridge
to print and sell
all manner of books
was granted by
Henry VIII in 1534.
The University has printed
and published continuously
since 1584.*

CAMBRIDGE UNIVERSITY PRESS
Cambridge
New York   New Rochelle
Melbourne   Sydney

Published by the Press Syndicate of the University of Cambridge
The Pitt Building, Trumpington Street, Cambridge CB2 1RP
32 East 57th Street, New York, NY 10022, USA
10 Stamford Road, Oakleigh, Melbourne 3166, Australia

© Schools Council Publications 1981
© SCDC Publications 1984

First published 1981
Third printing 1988

Printed in Great Britain by
David Green Printers Ltd, Kettering, Northants

ISBN 0 521 28217 9

Acknowledgements

The author and publisher would like to thank the following for permission to reproduce illustrations.

Bardo National Museum, Tunis front cover; Vatican Museums p. 7; The Trustees of the British Museum pp. 8, 13 below left, 14, 16 left, 18 left, 21 below, 29, 32 left, 47, 52 above, 57 below; National Museum of Wales pp. 9, 13 below right, 21 centre; Peter Reynolds pp. 10, 54 below left; Winchester City Museum p. 11; Bell and Hyman, taken from *The Gentleman's Magazine* 1788 p. 12; Museum of Antiquities of the University and Society of Antiquities, Newcastle-upon-Tyne p. 13 above left; John Webb photography p. 13 above right; Yorkshire Museum p. 15; The Warburg Institute p. 16 right; Musée Calvet, Avignon p. 17; Museum of London p. 18 right; Somerset County Museum p. 20 above; West Dorset Museum p. 20 below; Dorset Natural History and Archaeological Society in the Dorset County Museum, Dorset p. 21 above; Philip Dixon, University of Nottingham pp. 22 above, 56 below; Cambridge University Collection, copyright reserved pp. 22 below, 41, 54 above, 56 above, 60 above; Colchester and Essex Museum, pp. 26, 27, 66; Colchester Archaeological Trust p. 28; Society of Antiquaries of London pp. 32 above, 57 above, 60 below, 61; Mansell Collection pp. 34, 35, 37, 42, 44, 45, 46, 50, 67; Air photographs Index, Norfolk Archaeological Unit, photograph Derek Edwards p. 38 above; Mr Herbert Clegg and the Cumberland and Westmorland Antiquarian and Archaeological Society p. 38 below; The Society for the promotion of Roman Studies pp. 40, 59 below; Photographie Girandon p. 49; Barbara Malter pp. 52 below, 53 above; Wiltshire Archaeological and Natural History Society p. 53 below; Copyright Danebury Trust p. 54 below right; Department of the Environment, Crown copyright p. 55; Verulamium Museum, St Albans p. 58; German Archaeological Institute, Roman p. 59 above; Judges Ltd, Hastings p. 62 above; Sussex Archaeological Society p. 62 below; Nigel Sunter p. 63; Gloucester Museum p. 65; *The Roman Inscriptions of Britain*, vol. I by R. G. Collingwood and R. P. Wright (Oxford University Press, 1965) pp. 68, 69; Coventry Museum p.33.

Maps drawn by Reg Piggott

Contents

Core texts   **6**
  1 Britain, an unexplored land   6
  2 Julius Caesar's expeditions to Britain   7
  3 Gaius Caesar – a madman's escapade   12
  4 Gangling barbarians in a fog-bound land   13
  5 A traveller's tale   15
  6 Claudius' invasion   16
  7 King Cogidumnus   23
  8 Suetonius Paulinus and the Druids   23
  9 Boudica's rebellion   25
  10 The aftermath   31
  11 The Britons become romanised   33

Resources   **34**
Resources 1   More about the Roman army   34
Resources 2   More about the Britons   53
Resources 3   Making sense of Roman inscriptions   64

Greek and Roman writers   70
Some Roman emperors   72

Core texts

1 Britain, an unexplored land

> Until Julius Caesar's day, the Greeks and Romans had little first-hand knowledge of Britain but they found it especially interesting, because it was separated from the continent of Europe by sea. The ancients called this sea Oceanus, the great river which encircled the earth.

Britain, right at the very end of the earth.

Horace Odes

The stream of Oceanus, filled with large numbers of sea-monsters, dashes against the shores of the distant Britons.

Horace Odes

The spine-chilling sea and the Britons at the very end of the earth.

Catullus

The Britons, who are savage towards foreigners.

Horace Odes

> Romans of Caesar's time knew well how earlier Greek writers had described what lay west of the Pillars of Hercules (Straits of Gibraltar) where Oceanus began. Here, they said, the real world came to an end and the world of unknown peoples and mythical creatures began.

Odysseus' ship then reached the edge of the deep-flowing stream of Oceanus where the province and city of the Cimmerians are, shrouded in mist and cloud.

Homer Odyssey

Although I have tried to get hold of information, I have never been able to find out whether there is a sea that lies beyond the continent of Europe on the western and northern sides. Yet it cannot be denied that tin and amber do come to us from what one might call the ends of the earth. It is also clear that the northern parts of Europe are richest in gold, but we do not know how it is obtained. There is a story that one-eyed Arimaspeans steal the gold from the gryphons who guard it. But, for my part, I am reluctant to believe in men who have only one eye, but are in other ways exactly like us. In any case it seems to me to be true to say that the lands which lie on the edge of the inhabited earth produce the things which we value most greatly both for their scarcity and their beauty.

Herodotus

They say that the Phoenicians of Gades sailed with an east wind behind
them for four days from the Pillars of Hercules. They reached a desolate
spot, full of tangled seaweed which floats on the ebb tide, but which
disappears when the tide is in flood; and in it there are an enormous
number of fish, incredibly large and fat.

Pseudo-Aristotle

Note 34 Gades: Cadiz

A marble bust of Julius Caesar.

2 Julius Caesar's expeditions to Britain

The divine Julius was the first man ever to cross to Britain with an army.
He scared the inhabitants by beating them in battle and he captured the
coastal area. We must look upon Julius Caesar as the man who showed the
island to future generations, rather than bequeathed it.

Tacitus *Life of Agricola*

Caesar crosses Oceanus

Caesar was ready and when the weather was right he set sail at about the
third watch of the night. He ordered his cavalry to go by land to a harbour
along the coast, board the ships and then follow on. But the cavalry took
rather too long to do this. Caesar reached Britain at about the fourth hour
of the day. There he saw the armed forces of the enemy in full view along
the clifftops. So sheer were the cliffs which lined the coast, that missiles
could be thrown down from them straight onto the shore below.

Thinking that this place was unsuitable for disembarking his men, Caesar waited at anchor till the ninth hour for the rest of the fleet to arrive. In the meantime he called together his legates and tribunes to tell them what he had found out from his scout Volusenus and what he wanted done. He reminded them that in all battles, but especially in battles at sea, things can happen very quickly, and so they should be ready to carry out all orders immediately. Then he sent them away, and as soon as he obtained a favourable wind and tide he gave the signal and weighed anchor, moving forward about seven miles. He grounded the ships in a place where the shore was level and open.

An unfriendly reception

But the barbarians had realised what the Romans intended and had sent ahead their horsemen and charioteers (they always use these in battle). The rest of their forces had followed and were now in position to prevent our troops from disembarking. It therefore proved extremely difficult for our men to get out of their ships. The ships were so large that they had to heave to a good distance from the shore. The men were in a strange land, their hands were not free because they were loaded up with the great weight of their weapons and armour, yet they had to jump down from their ships, keep their balance in the cross-currents and fight the enemy all at the same time. By contrast the enemy had none of these problems and they knew the lie of the land very well. They stood either on dry land or moved forward a short way into the water and brazenly hurled missiles or whipped on their horses which were trained in such tactics. Our men were inexperienced in this kind of fighting and greatly alarmed. As a result they failed to push forward with the same alertness and vigour that they had always shown when fighting on dry land.

A British helmet, dated about 25 B.C. made of bronze, found in the River Thames at London. The tips of the horns are just over 41 cm apart.

A model of a British chariot, based on fragments found in Anglesey.

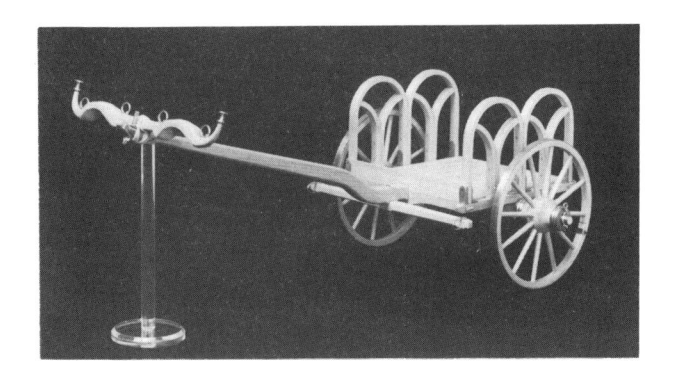

When Caesar realised this, he gave orders for the warships to pull out a little way from the cargo ships. The enemy was not used to warships and they were much more manoeuvrable. They were to row as quickly as possible and to station themselves on the enemy's unprotected flank. Then from that position they were to drive them off and clear them right away using slings, arrows and war-engines. The tactic proved to be a great help to our troops. For the barbarians were disturbed by the shape of the ships, by the beating of the oars and by the unfamiliar type of war-engines. They stood still in their tracks and then withdrew for a short distance. Our men still hesitated, mainly because of the deep water, but the eagle-bearer of the tenth legion offered a prayer to the gods, calling on them to look favourably upon the legion. Then he shouted, 'Jump down, lads, you don't want to betray your eagle to the enemy, do you? At least I will have done my bit for the republic and for my commander.' Then he dived from the ship and began carrying the eagle towards the enemy. At this our men urged one another not to allow such a disgrace to take place and all leapt down from the ships together. When the troops on the nearest ships saw them, they did the same and waded in to meet the enemy.

The fighting was fierce on both sides, but our men were in complete disorder. As they jumped down each man formed up behind the first standard he saw and so they could not organise a proper attack because they were not in their usual formation. But the enemy knew exactly where the water was shallowest. Whenever they spotted a group of our men jumping down one by one from a ship and struggling along they galloped up and overpowered them, and whenever they saw a large block of Romans they drove round to their exposed side and hurled javelins at them. When Caesar realised what was happening he had the rowing boats of the warships and the reconnaissance craft filled up with soldiers and sent them to help any of our men in difficulties.

The moment our men got a steady foothold on dry land they made a mass charge and put the enemy to flight. But they were unable to pursue them very far, because the cavalry had not been able to keep on course and reach the island. This was the only thing Caesar needed to help him be as successful as usual.

Julius Caesar   *The Gallic War*

Letters from home

    Two letters referring to Caesar's second expedition.

You may have learned to be careful in dealing with your clients, but make sure in Britain that you are not taken for a ride by those charioteers!
                      Cicero writing to C. Trebatius Testa in May 54 B.C.

I am surprised that I do not receive letters from you as often as I do from my brother Quintus. I hear that there is not a scrap of gold or silver in Britain. If that is the case, I suggest you capture a chariot and drive back here as soon as you can.
                      Cicero writing to Trebatius in the same month.

How the Britons live

    Julius Caesar's account of his two expeditions to Britain in 55 and 54 B.C. include some first impressions of the island and its inhabitants.

The inland part of Britain is inhabited by tribes which are, according to their own folklore, natives of the island; along the coast on the other hand are those who crossed over from Belgian Gaul to plunder and make war. Almost all these Gauls are known by the names of the states they came from. After invading the island they made their home there and began to cultivate the land.

    The population of the island is countless. Houses rather like those in Gaul are to be seen everywhere and there are enormous numbers of cattle.

A British iron age roundhouse, reconstructed on the evidence of excavated remains.

Iron currency bars found on Worthy Down, Hampshire.

They use either bronze or gold coinage. Sometimes instead of coined money they use iron bars of a standard weight. In the interior of the island there is tin to be found, and in coastal areas iron, but there is only a small amount of it. They use imported bronze. There is timber of every kind, as in Gaul, except for beech and fir trees. They do not consider it right to eat hare, chickens or geese, and they breed them for their amusement only. The weather is milder than in Gaul and the cold season is less severe.

The natural shape of the island is triangular and one of the sides lies facing Gaul. One corner of this side is Cantium, where almost all the ships from Gaul come in to land. Cantium faces east and the other corner which is lower down points towards the south. This side is about 500 miles long.

The second side runs in the direction of Spain and the west, where Hibernia lies. This is an island which is thought to be half the size of Britain and which lies the same distance from Britain as Britain is from Gaul. Halfway across is an island called Mona. There are also thought to be many smaller islands which lie nearer the coast of Britain. Some writers have suggested that in the middle of winter there is continual night there for thirty whole days. We could not find out anything about this from our enquiries, but by using a water-clock we noted that the nights were shorter than on the continent. The length of this side is 700 miles according to local opinion.

The third side points northwards and has no land lying opposite it. The corner on that side, however, generally faces Germany. This side is supposed to be 800 miles long, thus making the whole island 2,000 miles all the way round.

Of all the Britons, the inhabitants of Cantium, which is on the coast, are by far the most civilised and are very little different from the Gauls in their way of life. Most of those who live inland do not sow grain but live on milk and meat and dress in animal skins. All the Britons, certainly, dye themselves with woad which produces a blue dye and makes them look wild in battle. They wear their hair long and shave every part of their body except the head and upper lip. Wives are shared by groups of ten or twelve men especially by brothers or by fathers and sons, but the children born are reckoned to belong to the first husband the woman takes up with.

Julius Caesar   *The Gallic War*

3 Gaius Caesar—a madman's escapade

The next man who thought of invading Britain was the mad Emperor Gaius Caesar, known as Caligula. This is what Suetonius tells us of his plans.

He gathered great numbers of soldiers and made tremendous preparations. He drew up his army in full battle order along the shore of Oceanus and placed his *ballistae* and his siege engines in position as if he intended to declare war. No one had any idea at all what he had in mind. Suddenly he gave his order: 'Pick up sea shells, men; stuff your helmets and your tunics with them! These shells are plunder we have won from Oceanus; we will give them to the Capitol and to the Palatine.' He commemorated this 'victory' by building a tall lighthouse which, like the Pharos at Alexandria, has fires that burn all the time to guide ships at night.

Suetonius *Life of Caligula*

Notes 4 shore of Oceanus: thought to be near Boulogne in northern France
5 *ballistae:* artillery

The lighthouse in this old drawing is thought to be the one built by Gaius at Boulogne. It was destroyed in 1544.

4 Gangling barbarians in a fog-bound land

This is how Strabo, writing at the time of Augustus, described the Britons.

Most of the island is flat and covered in forests though there are many hilly areas.

Grain, cattle, gold, silver and iron are found on the island. They are exported together with hides, slaves and excellent hunting dogs. The Gauls use these and their own dogs in warfare. 5

right: Bronze model of a hunting terrier, found in a well at a fort on Hadrian's wall.

far right: Bronze model of a wolfhound found at the Roman site at Lydney, in Gloucestershire.

The Britons are taller than the Gauls, their hair is not so yellow and their bodies are more gangling. To give some idea of their size, I saw some of them in Rome, just young boys, but they towered half a foot above the tallest people there. What is more they were bandy-legged and their bodies all crooked. 10

left: A British shield, dated to before the Claudian invasion, found in the river Witham, near Lincoln.

right: A British slave chain of similar date, found in Wales.

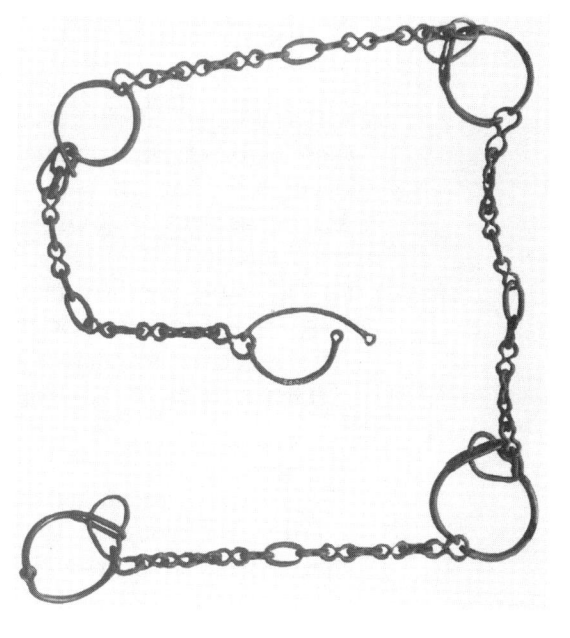

Two sides of a British gold coin minted at Camulodunum, about A.D. 10-20.

A British torque, dated to about 20 B.C., found in Norfolk.

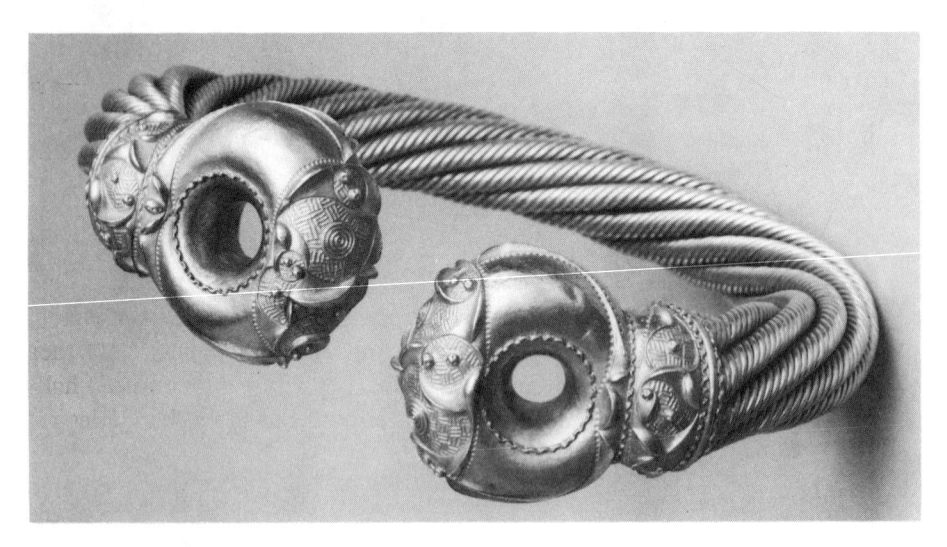

Their way of life is a bit like that of the Gauls but much cruder and more barbaric. For example, although they have plenty of milk some of them do not know how to make cheese, nor do they know anything about keeping gardens or farms. In war they use mainly chariots just as some of the Gauls do.

Their cities are the forests. They cut down the trees and fence in a large round space. In this enclosure they build their huts and corral their cattle, but they do not stay in any one place for very long.

They have more rain than snow and on days when there is no rain the fog hangs about for so long that the sun shines for only three or four hours around midday.

Apart from some other small islands around Britain there is a large one called Ierne. About this island I can say nothing definitely except that the inhabitants are fiercer than the Britons and that they are man-eaters.

Adapted from Strabo *Geography*

5 A traveller's tale

Two greatly respected men, who had come from opposite ends of the inhabited earth, met at Delphi in the mainland of Greece, probably in A.D. 83. They were Demetrius the school teacher, who was on his way back home from Britain to Tarsus, and Cleombrotus of Sparta. This was Demetrius' story.

Among the islands that lie just off the coast of Britain are many scattered and deserted islands. Some of these are called by the names of spirits and heroes.

On the order of the emperor, I took part in an expedition to explore and to survey the nearest of these islands, which had only a few inhabitants who were all thought by the Britons to be holy men not to be interfered with on any account. Shortly after we arrived a great storm gathered and Zeus sent many omens; winds rushed down on the face of the earth and there were violent outbreaks of thunder and lightning. When they had died down, the islanders said that it must have been the passing of one of the great men: 'For' they claimed 'the light of a lamp does not frighten anyone while it is burning, but when it is put out many people find it upsetting. In the same way the souls of the great burn brightly, showing goodwill but no harm to others, but when they die and their souls pass away, as has just happened, there are wind and rain storms. Often the air becomes poisoned with deadly disease.'

They also claimed that in that part of the world is one particular island, where Cronos is kept prisoner by Briareus while he sleeps. For his sleep has been devised as a means of chaining him down, and all round him are many spirits who act as attendants and servants.

Plutarch *Moralia*

Notes 22 Cronos: the father of Zeus
22 Briareus: a hundred-handed giant

A bronze plate found at York in 1840, punched with Greek lettering. The inscription means 'To Oceanus and Tethys (set up by) Demetrius.'

15

left: Two sides of a gold coin of Verica, son of Commius. Verica is generally identified with the Bericus of Dio Cassius (see below).

right: A bronze head of the Emperor Claudius, found in the river Alde, Suffolk.

6 Claudius' invasion

The Emperor Claudius' expedition in A.D. 43 was the first serious attempt by the Romans to follow the lead given by Julius Caesar.

Aulus Plautius, a greatly respected senator, commanded an expedition against Britain. For a certain Bericus, who had been driven out of the island during an uprising, had persuaded Claudius to send a force there. So Plautius was leading the company. However, he had great difficulty in getting his army to go any further than the coast of Gaul, for his soldiers objected violently to campaigning beyond the limits of the known world and would not obey his orders. Claudius sent his freedman Narcissus to deal with the situation. Narcissus climbed onto the platform and tried to address the men. They simply grew angrier and would not allow him to speak. Then suddenly they all saw the funny side of it and shouted out 'Io Saturnalia!' (This is what people shout at the festival of Saturn when slaves dress up in their masters' clothes and celebrate.) The soldiers now obeyed Plautius' orders without further argument. But the delay meant that it was now late in the season.

Aulus Plautius' campaign

Plautius split his men into three groups to cross the straits. This was to make sure that they were not all prevented from landing as they might have been if they went in one fleet. During the voyage across, the ships were blown off course and the troops became downhearted. But they cheered up when they saw a flash of light shoot across the sky from east to west – the direction in which they were sailing. So they reached the island – but there was no one waiting to meet them. The Britons had received wrong information and were not expecting them! When the Britons did assemble, they did not come in close ranks, but scattered into swamps and forests, hoping to wear out the Romans and cause them to achieve nothing, as in Julius Caesar's day.

Plautius now had great difficulty tracking them down. In the end he caught up with the brothers Caratacus and Togodumnus, chieftains of the Catuvellauni tribe. He defeated them and put them to flight.

The Britons were not free and independent, but were divided into tribes under various kings. Now part of the Bodunni tribe, who had been ruled by the Catuvellauni, surrendered. Plautius left a garrison in their lands and marched on until he reached a river. The barbarians did not think that the Romans would be able to cross without a bridge and so they camped without taking proper care on the opposite bank. Plautius sent across a unit of Gauls. These men were used to swimming in full armour across the strongest currents. They took the enemy by surprise, but instead of attacking the men they set about wounding the horses that pulled the chariots. In the chaos that followed not even the charioteers could escape.

A stone statue of a Gallic auxiliary soldier, found in France.

Then Plautius sent across Flavius Vespasianus (the future emperor) and his brother Sabinus, his second-in-command. They took the enemy by surprise, killing many of them. The rest of the Britons, however, did not run away, but attacked again the next day. The battle was indecisive until C. Hosidius Geta, who was very nearly taken prisoner, managed to beat back the barbarians completely. For this he was later awarded the *ornamenta triumphalia* even though he was not of consular rank.

The Britons then withdrew to the River Tamesis to a point near where it flows into Oceanus and where a lake is formed at high tide. This they crossed easily because they knew where the firm ground and the fording-places were. But the Romans were not so successful when they tried to follow. However, the Gauls again swam across while some others got over by means of a bridge a little way upstream. After this they attacked the barbarians from several sides at once and killed many of them. In chasing after the enemy, they did not look where they were going, and so landed in swampy ground which was impossible to get out of and lost a large number of men.

A bronze legionary helmet of standard type for the first century A.D.

A Roman iron dagger and sheath frame, found in London.

Shortly after this Togodumnus was killed. This made the Britons even more determined not to give up. They organised themselves for revenge. Because of the difficulties Plautius had run into at the River Tamesis, he began to fear what would happen if he advanced any further. So he decided to hold on to what he had already won and to send for Claudius. He had been instructed to do this if he met any particularly strong resistance. In fact Claudius was ready waiting to come with a large army, well equipped with armaments including elephants.

The emperor takes over command of the army

When the news reached him, Claudius put his fellow consul L. Vitellius in charge of home affairs including the command of the army. He then set out himself on his expedition. He sailed down the river to Ostia and from there he followed the coast to Massilia. From that point he travelled partly by land and partly along the rivers. He reached Oceanus and crossed over to Britain and joined the legions that were waiting for him on the Tamesis. He took charge of the troops and crossed the river. Then he attacked the barbarians who had come together to meet him as he advanced. He defeated them in battle and captured Camulodunum, the capital of Cunobelin.

Evidence for Claudius' invasion

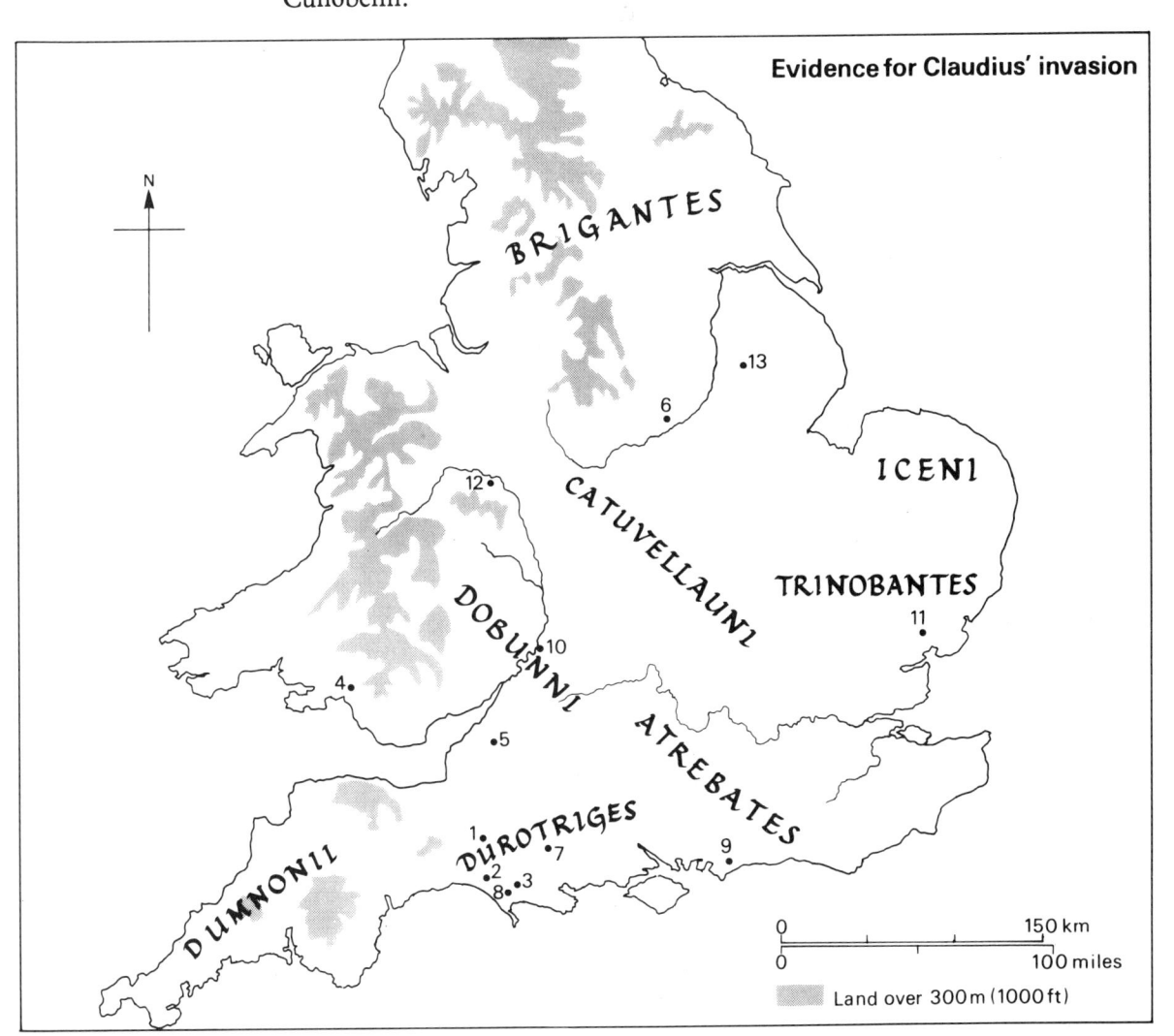

This map shows places where archaeological evidence for Claudius' invasion has been found. The places are marked by numbers, which correspond to numbered 'clues' in this book. **Clues 1–7** are between pages 20 and 22, and **Clues 8–13** are between pages 60 and 69. Study the clues to find out what each piece of evidence is and the name of the place on the map where it was found.

From then on he won over to his side many tribes; some surrendered to him after negotiations, but others were forced to give in. Claudius was hailed as *Imperator* on several occasions, although it was not possible for anyone to be given this title more than once during the same war. All tribes that surrendered were made to hand over all their weapons to Plautius. Claudius gave instructions that all the remaining parts of Britain were to be conquered. He then hurried back to Rome sending ahead news of his victory. The senate, on learning of his success, awarded him the title of 'Britannicus' and gave him permission to celebrate a triumph. It was also agreed that a festival should be held every year to celebrate the event. They also set up two triumphal arches, one in Rome and one in Gaul because it was from that country that Claudius had set sail when he crossed over to Britain.

Dio Cassius

Note 71 Massilia: Marseilles

Clue 1 Roman scale armour found at Ham Hill, Somerset.

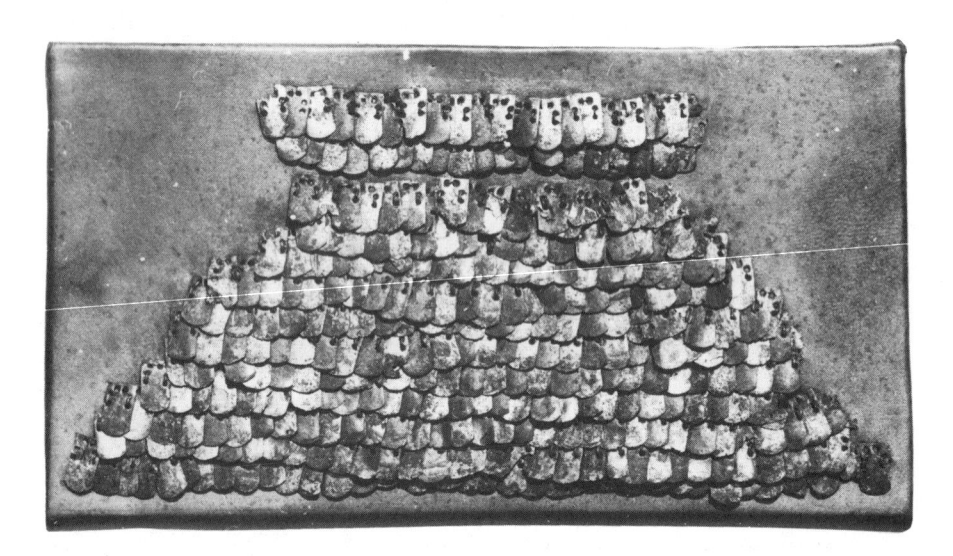

Clue 2 Fragment of a Roman dagger scabbard inlaid with gold, found at the British fort of Waddon Hill, in Dorset.

Clue 3 A Roman soldier's belt mount, decorated with enamel inlay. It was found at Dorchester in Dorset.

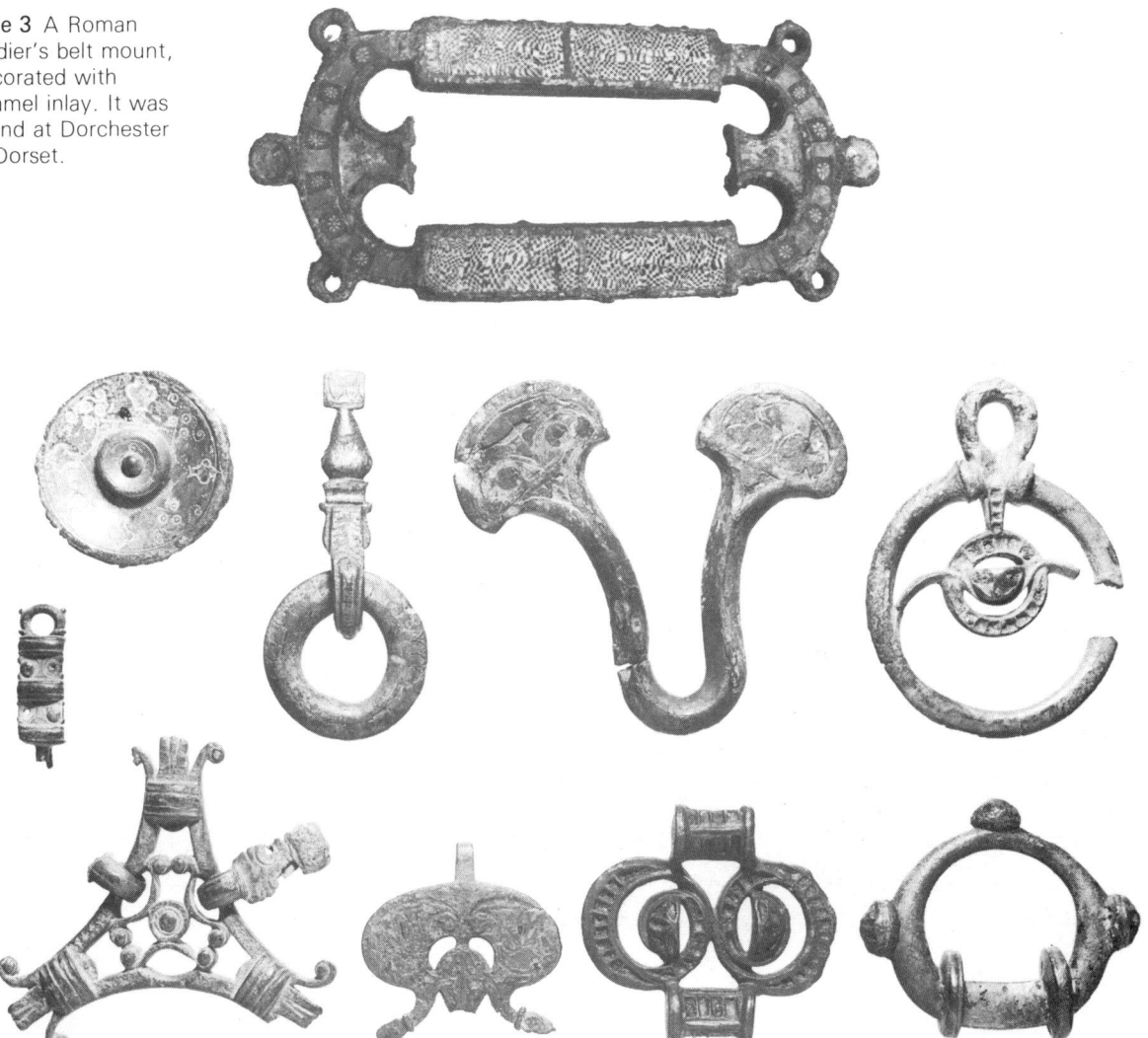

above: **Clue 4** A hoard of metal objects, including Roman cavalry equipment, probably made by British craftsmen for the Roman army. They were found at Nant-y-Cefn, in the Vale of Neath, South Wales.

below: **Clue 5** A Roman lead pig stamped BRITANNIC. AVG. FI (meaning 'product of Britannicus, son of Augustus'). It was found at Blagdon on the northern Mendip hills, in Avon.

Clue 6 A Roman soldier's mess tin made of bronze, from Broxtowe, Nottingham.

After Vespasian was transferred to Britain, he fought battles with the enemy. He conquered two very powerful tribes, more than twenty *oppida* and the island of Vectis which lies near the coast of Britain. He did this partly under the command of Aulus Plautius, partly under Claudius himself. For these victories Vespasian was awarded the *ornamenta triumphalia*.

Suetonius   *Life of Vespasian*

Note 93 *oppida:* here, Celtic settlements or forts

Clue 7 A British hill fort at Hod Hill, Dorset, with a Roman auxiliary fort inside.

7 King Cogidumnus

After their first military successes the Romans set about turning Britain into a province of the empire. They were by this time very experienced in making use of colonies of their own veteran soldiers and friendly native chieftains to help them in their task. Cogidumnus was one such client-king who continued to rule his own people in return for loyalty to the Romans.

The next governor of Britain after Aulus Plautius was Ostorius Scapula. Each man was in his own way a distinguished soldier. The nearest part of Britain was gradually made into a province. A *colonia* of veteran soldiers was set up there. Some tribal states were handed over to King Cogidumnus who has remained completely loyal down to our own times. This is a good example of how we Romans use even kings to help us make people slaves.

Tacitus *Life of Agricola*

Note 8 *colonia:* new town

8 Suetonius Paulinus and the Druids

The campaign

During the years following Claudius' invasion the Romans extended their military control into south-west Britain, Wales and as far as the River Humber (see map p.25). Continued resistance to the Roman army was ruthlessly dealt with.

Suetonius Paulinus was put in charge of Britain . . . He planned an attack on the island of Mona. This island had a large population and was full of refugees. The sea between the island and the mainland is shallow and dangerous, so Paulinus built a fleet of flat-bottomed boats for ferrying the infantry across. The cavalrymen followed behind, walking alongside their horses and swimming when the sea became deeper.

Before them on the shore stood the enemy, lined up in a densely packed body bristling with weapons. Women wove their way in and out of the battle lines. They looked just like Furies dressed in black robes, with their hair all loose, and brandishing torches. At the same time a circle of Druids raised their hands to heaven, screaming out terrible curses. The troops were dumbfounded by this strange spectacle. They stood in their tracks as though paralysed and left themselves exposed to the enemy fire. But after being reassured by their general, they urged one another not to be frightened by a band of fanatical women. Then they charged forward behind their standards. They hacked down anyone who tried to stop them and then enveloped the enemy in the flames of their own torches. The next step was to station a garrison among the conquered population and to destroy the groves which were dedicated to their savage and superstitious practices. For it is part of their religion to soak their altars with the blood of their prisoners and to consult their gods by inspecting human entrails.

Tacitus *Annals*

The Druids

> Many years earlier Julius Caesar had recognised the powerful influence of the Druids in Gaul.

The Druids' job is to perform sacrifices, worship the gods and interpret religious matters. They act as judges in almost all public and private disputes. If any crime is committed, for example, if there is murder or if there is an argument over who gets what when somebody has died or over the boundary between one person's land and another's, it is the Druids' job to decide the matter. They decide what rewards and punishments are to be given out. If anyone fails to abide by their decision, he is banned from taking part in sacrifices, which is a very serious matter. Those that are banned are thought to be impious and wicked men. Everyone moves out of their way. No one wants to meet them or talk to them for fear of coming to any harm from being in contact with them. Justice is not granted to them when they seek it, nor is any honour given to them.

There is one chief Druid who is the most important of them all. When he dies another outstanding Druid takes his place or, if there are several contenders, they hold an election among themselves or even fight the matter out. At certain times of the year those Druids meet in the land of the Carnutes whose territory is thought to be the very centre of Gaul and hold their conference in a sacred place. To this place come all those who have disputes to settle and they abide by the decisions and judgements of the Druids. It is thought that the Druids' way of life was brought over from Britain to Gaul. Today anyone who wants to find out more exactly what the Druids are like goes across to Britain.

The Druids usually take no part in war. They do not pay war taxes like everyone else and they are exempted from military service and other duties. Many young men are tempted by these privileges and volunteer to go for training as Druids. Many are sent by their parents or by relatives. It is said that in the Druids' schools they have to learn to recite many lines of verse by heart, so that some people spend twenty years training. They do not think it right to put these verses down in writing, although they use Greek letters for their public and private accounts. In my opinion, they do this for two reasons: firstly, they do not want everyone to know about their way of life; secondly, they do not want those who learn it to rely on writing as this would mean that they would not keep their memories in training. (In fact it usually happens that although writing is useful it tends to make the student less alert and his memory less reliable.)

Their main teaching is that souls do not die but when a man dies his soul passes to someone else. This belief helps to make them brave, as they do not need to fear death. In addition, they are always discussing such matters as the stars and their movements, the size of the universe and the earth, the nature of the universe and power of the immortal gods. And they pass on this learning to the younger generation.

Julius Caesar   *The Gallic War*

Britain at the time of the Boudican rebellion

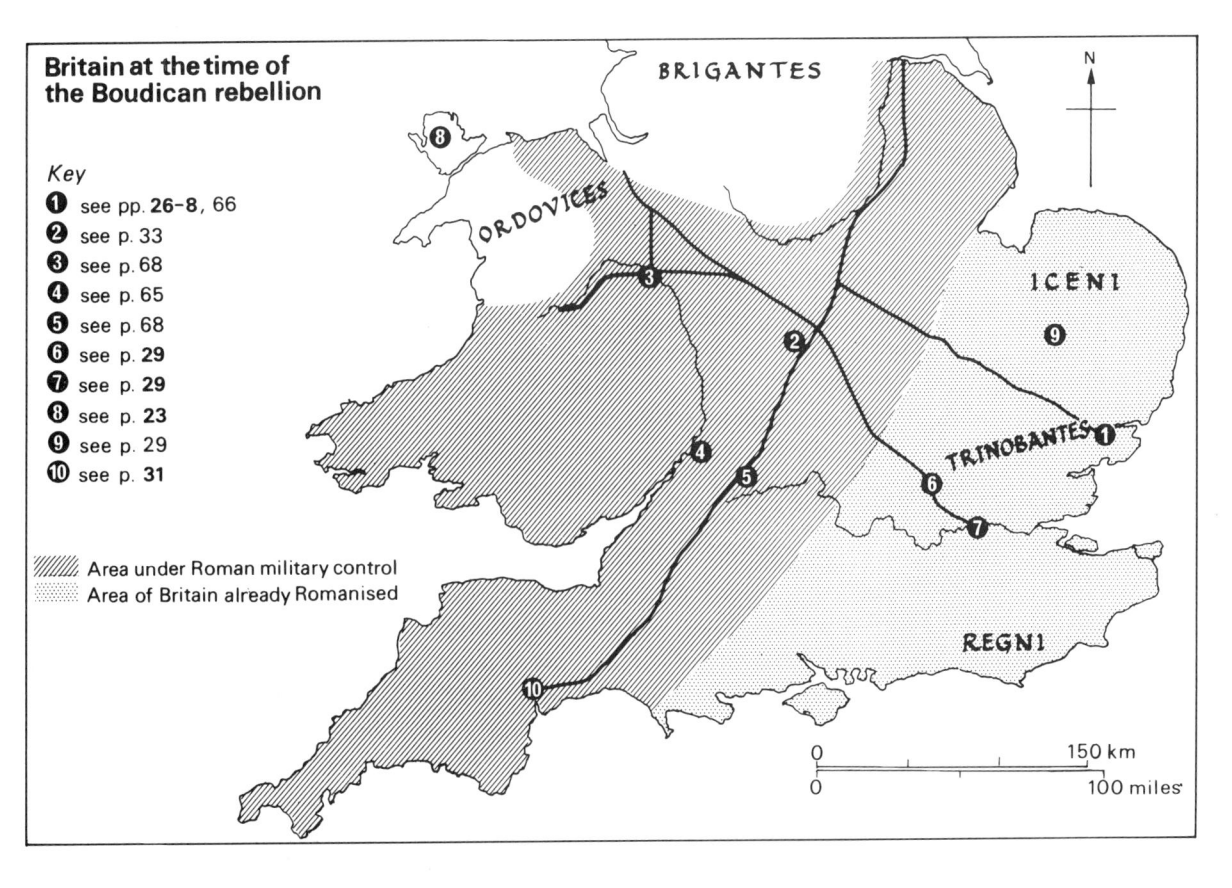

Key
❶ see pp. 26-8, 66
❷ see p. 33
❸ see p. 68
❹ see p. 65
❺ see p. 68
❻ see p. 29
❼ see p. 29
❽ see p. 23
❾ see p. 29
❿ see p. 31

▨ Area under Roman military control
▦ Area of Britain already Romanised

The numbered dots on the map show either places mentioned in the text or places where evidence has been found that may be connected with the Boudican rebellion. The page references in the key are the pages where you can find this information. (Those in heavy type are references to texts and those in ordinary type are references to pictures.) Draw your own map and name the places. Can you work out the movements of the Roman troops and British rebels during the uprising?

9 Boudica's rebellion

Prasutagus, tribal chieftain of the Iceni, had ruled his people as a client-king like Cogidumnus. After Prasutagus' death, his wife Boudica led a rebellion against the Romans. Suetonius Paulinus, who was still busy in Mona at the time, received news that the province had suddenly revolted.

Two cities were sacked, 80,000 Romans and their allies were killed, and the island was lost to the Romans. What made matters worse was that all this ruin was brought about by a woman; this in itself was something to be deeply ashamed of.

This woman was Boudica, a Briton of royal family. The rebels considered her to be their ablest leader. She was much more intelligent than women usually are. She was very tall, and she looked terrifying with a fierce glint in her eyes and with a raucous voice. A great mass of startling yellow hair hung down to her hips. Around her neck she had a huge torque of gold and she wore a dress of many colours with a thin cloak over it pinned together with a brooch. This was the way she normally dressed. She had gathered together an army of about 120,000 men.

Dio Cassius

Note 13 torque: see photograph page 14

How the rebellion started

Boudica's husband, Prasutagus, had been the king of the Iceni. He lived a long life and was famous for his great wealth. In his will he had named Caesar and his two daughters as co-heirs. He did this thinking that it would mean that his kingdom and his family would be safe when he died. What happened was quite the opposite, for his kingdom was ravaged by centurions and his house by slaves, just as if they were the spoils of war.

To begin with Boudica was flogged and her daughters were raped. It was as if the whole territory had been presented to the Romans as a gift. All the chief men of the Iceni had their ancestral farms taken away from them and the king's own family were treated like slaves. Infuriated by these outrages and by the fear of worse to come now that the area had been made part of the province, they urged the Trinobantes to join them along with other tribes which were not yet broken by slavery and which were plotting with them to get back their freedom. They particularly hated the Roman veterans who had recently been settled at Camulodunum. These veterans had evicted the natives from their own homes, and had driven people from their own lands calling them 'captives' and 'slaves'. They were encouraged in this by the soldiers who looked forward to enjoying the same benefits

A reconstruction of the temple of Claudius at Camulodunum.

The vault of the temple of Claudius.

Some burnt dates, from the destruction of Camulodunum.

themselves when they retired. To make matters worse the temple which had been built in honour of the divine Claudius constantly stared them in the face as a stronghold of permanent tyranny. Natives were chosen to be priests of this temple and they were expected to pour all their wealth into doing the job. There did not seem to be any great difficulty in destroying the settlement, for it had no walls to protect it. That was a point which our Roman generals had neglected. They had not bothered to build any, for they thought more of luxuries than of necessities.

Now for no obvious reason, the statue of Victory at Camulodunum fell with its back turned as if it was in retreat from the enemy. Women ran mad with panic wailing 'Death! Death! The end is near!' They said that they had heard strange wild groans coming from the senate house while the theatre echoed with shrieks and howls. They said they had seen a strange vision under the waters of Tamesis – the *colonia* tumbled in ruins. Oceanus

Burnt pottery excavated from the charred remains of Camulodunum.

ran blood-red and as the tide ebbed it left behind shapes like the corpses of men. All these signs gave the Britons hope, but the veterans became more and more alarmed. Suetonius was a long way away so they sent to the Procurator Catus Decianus for help. He sent no more than 200 men, who did not even have the proper equipment. Added to this there was only a small body of troops in the town. The people of the *colonia* relied on the protection of the temple; thwarted in their plans by secret supporters of the rebellion they did not build a defensive ditch and bank. They did not even evacuate the elderly and the women and thus leave younger men behind to do the fighting. As careless as if they were living in complete peace, they were encircled by a large crowd of barbarians. Everything was ransacked or set on fire during the first attack. Only the temple in which the troops were stationed in full force managed to hold out in a two-day siege, before it too was overthrown.

The victorious Britons then turned to meet Petilius Cerialis, legate of the ninth legion, who was on his way bringing help. His troops were driven back and then all the foot-soldiers he had with him were slaughtered to a man. Cerialis got back to his camp with the cavalry and took cover behind his defences. The Procurator Catus Decianus, deeply upset by this disaster and by the hatred of Roman rule that his rapacious policy had turned into war, crossed over in terror to Gaul.

Note 54 Procurator: official in charge of imperial property and revenue in Britain

Two cups from a hoard of early Roman silver found in the land of the Iceni. The cups were found in fragments and have been restored.

Suetonius Paulinus marches south

Suetonius on the other hand was quite unperturbed and marched straight through the middle of the rebel-held lands to Londinium. Although this place did not have the distinction of being a *colonia*, it was nevertheless a bustling community, important for its merchants and its trade. When he arrived there he was not sure whether to make it a base for his operations. But, after considering how small his own forces were and the price that Petilius Cerialis had paid for acting rashly, he decided to give up the town of Londinium in order to save the province as a whole.

    He remained adamant in spite of the cries and tears of the inhabitants as they begged for help. He gave the signal for everyone to leave and allowed the inhabitants to join his army on the march. But those who stayed behind because they were women or too elderly or because they were too attached to the town were slaughtered by the enemy. The same disaster took place at the Roman city of Verulamium. For the barbarians with their usual love of plunder and their dislike of hard work ignored the forts and armed settlements and concentrated on those sites which were richest and where the defenders were less well protected. It is known that nearly 70,000 Roman citizens and their allies died in the places mentioned. For the enemy had no interest in taking or selling prisoners or in any other of the usual trade connected with war. Instead they were hell-bent on bloodshed and hangings, on burning and crucifying. It was as though they realised the day of reckoning would come, but they were determined to have their revenge first.

The final confrontation

Suetonius had with him the fourteenth legion together with part of the twentieth. There were also auxiliary troops from the nearest forts. This gave him about 10,000 men altogether. He prepared to attack without further delay and to fight a pitched battle. He chose a site which was approached by a narrow valley and which was hemmed in at the far end by a wood. He sent out scouts to make sure that there were no enemy in the rear and to check that there was nowhere in the plain before him where they could set up an ambush. He ordered his legionaries to bunch up in close formation and surrounded them with his light-armed troops. On each wing he massed the cavalry.

The Britons, on the other hand, dotted all over the place in groups of foot-soldiers and horsemen, were dashing around. There were more of them than had ever been seen before. They were so confident that they had even brought their wives to see them win the battle and had stationed them in waggons parked at the edge of the battlefield.

Boudica drove around to each of the tribes in turn with her daughters in front of her and cried, 'We Britons are used to fighting under women generals. I am descended from great men, but today I am not fighting for my kingdom or for my family fortunes. I am fighting as an ordinary woman; as one who has lost her freedom, who has been flogged, whose daughters have been outraged. Roman demands have reached such a point that not even the bodies of the elderly or of children are spared. But now the gods are on our side. They will help us to have our just revenge. One legion that dared to face us has already been destroyed. The others are hiding in their camps or looking round for a chance to escape. They will never be able to bear the roaring and shouting of all our thousands, not to mention our attack. If you think how many there are of you and the reasons for us being at war, then you must either win this battle or die. This is what I, a woman, am resolved to do. Let the men live and live as slaves, if they will.'

Even Suetonius at this critical stage addressed his troops, in spite of the trust which he placed in the courage of his men. This is what he said.

'Take no notice of the roars of the enemy and their empty threats: there are more women than men in their ranks. They are unwarlike and have no weapons. The moment they see the steel blades and the courage of an enemy that has beaten them so often, they will turn tail and run. Even in an army composed of many legions there are few who win battle honours. Just think what added glory awaits you as a much smaller band of men if you win the reputation of a whole army! Just keep in close formation, throw your javelins and use your shield bosses to knock them down and your swords to kill them. Forget about plundering: when you have beaten them, everything will be yours.' Suetonius' veteran soldiers with their long experience of battle were all keen and ready to throw their javelins at a moment's notice. They were so fired by their commander's words that Suetonius had no doubt in his mind and gave the signal for battle to begin.

To begin with the legions stood where they were, keeping to the narrow valley for protection. When the enemy came closer, they threw their javelins with accurate aim and then rushed forward in a wedge formation. The auxiliaries charged in the same way and the cavalry with their spears at the ready broke down all who resisted them. The rest of the Britons fled, although it was not easy because the line of waggons blocked their way. The troops showed no mercy even to the women. The pack-animals had been killed by flying weapons and their bodies made the pile of dead even larger. It was a glorious victory, like those of earlier days: according to some accounts, a few less than 80,000 Britons perished but there were only 400 or so dead on our side with as many again injured. Boudica ended her life by taking poison.

When the camp prefect of the second legion, Poenius Postumus, heard of the other two legions' success, he stabbed himself to death. He realised that he had cheated his men of their share in the victory and that he had broken regulations by disobeying his commander's instructions.

Tacitus *Annals*

Note 154 Poenius Postumus would have been third in command of the legion, which was by this date based at Exeter. Tacitus does not tell us any more about this episode.

10 The aftermath

Suetonius then brought the whole army together and kept it under canvas to finish the war. Tribes that were still hostile or not openly loyal were attacked and their villages burnt. The Britons' worst hardship was famine. They had not bothered to sow their crops – rather they had concentrated on the war all the summer, thinking that in the end they would be able to use our supplies.

By now Julius Classicianus had been sent out to replace Catus Decianus. Classicianus was on bad terms with Suetonius, and let his personal feelings come before the national interest. He let it be known that the Britons should wait for a new legate – one who would show some kindness, and not go about with the arrogance of a conqueror. This only made the headstrong British tribes more resentful against Suetonius and less interested in peace. Classicianus also sent a report to Rome. He said there would be no hope of finishing the war, unless Suetonius was replaced. His failures, it was argued, were a result of his own perverted character; his successes were entirely a matter of luck.

So Nero sent off one of his freedmen, Polyclitus, to assess the situation in Britain. Nero was relying on Polyclitus' influence to sort out the differences between the governor and procurator – and also to make the rebellious Britons more interested in peace. Polyclitus travelled with a huge escort – Italy and Gaul could barely support him with all his followers. Then he crossed Oceanus, and he even managed to make our soldiers afraid of him. However, the enemy simply laughed at him. They still knew what liberty was. As yet, they had not realised just how much power freedmen could have. They were amazed that a commander and an army which had won such a great war should let themselves be treated like slaves.

However, in his report to the emperor, Polyclitus toned down all this and Suetonius was kept on as governor. Some time later he lost a few ships and their rowers near the coast. On the pretext that he was prolonging the war, he was ordered to hand over the command of the army to Petronius Turpilianus, who had just finished his term as consul. He was completely idle, and yet he thought it was right to call this idleness 'peace'.

Tacitus *Annals*

Note 17 Nero: emperor at the time of the rebellion

A stone from Classicianus' tomb which was reused as a foundation stone in London wall.

To the Manes of Gaius Julius Alpinus Classicianus, son of Gaius, of the Fabian voting tribe . . .

Procurator of the province of Britain. His wife, Julia Pacata, daughter of Indus has this set up.

The reconstructed tombstone of Classicianus. The missing central section probably listed his previous appointments.

The auxiliary Roman fort at 'The Lunt', Baginton, near Coventry, has been excavated. The fort is dated to between A.D. 60 and A.D. 74. Its construction must be associated with the aftermath of the Boudican rebellion. The picture shows the reconstructed gateway and defences.

11 The Britons become romanised

Twenty years after Boudica's rebellion, Gnaeus Iulius Agricola, governor of Britain, and his army campaigned in the summer months to extend Roman control to the northern parts of the island.

The winter that followed was spent putting some useful schemes into operation. The population of Britain was scattered and uncivilised and so always ready to fight. In order to get the Britons to live in peace enjoying life's pleasures, Agricola encouraged individuals and helped local communities to build temples, *fora* and houses. He praised hard workers and scolded the lazy. So competing for honours replaced compulsion. Further, he trained the sons of tribal chieftains in the liberal arts. He made it clear that he preferred British natural ability to the trained skills of the Gauls. So it was that a people who had at first rejected the Latin language became keen to speak it fluently. In the same way, our dress became popular and the toga came into fashion.

Gradually, the Britons were led astray. They were tempted into adopting such vices as porticoes, baths and sumptuous dinner-parties. The uneducated natives spoke of such novelties as 'civilisation' when really it was part of their enslavement!

Tacitus *Life of Agricola*

Note 8 *fora:* plural of forum, the central part of any Roman town

Resources

Resources 1 More about the Roman army

1.1 Recruits

Choosing recruits for the army

Those whose job it is to choose new recruits should be particularly careful to examine their faces, their eyes and the shape of their limbs and to see that they are likely to make good soldiers. For the authority of experts has shown that choosing men is just like choosing horses and dogs. There are certain clues, which tell you whether or not they are likely to be any good. Even in the case of bee keeping, Virgil the famous writer of Mantua tells us: 'There are two sorts of bee. One is better than the other, fine looking and bright with shining scales. The other sort is scruffy to look at through its own life of laziness. It is an inferior type which trails along with a sagging belly.'

So a young soldier who is chosen for the work of Mars should have alert eyes and should hold his head upright. The recruit should be broad-chested with powerful shoulders and brawny arms. His fingers should be long rather than short. He should not be pot-bellied or have a fat bottom. His calves and feet should not be flabby; instead they should be made entirely of tough sinew. When you find all these qualities in a recruit, you can afford to take him even if he is a little on the short side. It is better for soldiers to be strong rather than tall.

It follows that in choosing or rejecting recruits, it is important to find out what trade they have been following. Fishermen, birdcatchers, sweet-makers, weavers and all those who do the kind of jobs that women normally do should be kept away from the army. On the other hand, smiths, carpenters, butchers and hunters of deer and wild boars are the most suitable kind of recruit. The whole well-being of the Roman state depends on the kind of recruits you choose; so this is why you must choose men who are outstanding not only in body but also in mind. This job of selection is of such great importance that it must be taken very seriously and not just left to anyone to carry out.

Vegetius

Recruits learn how to fight with a sword

The Romans train their recruits in the following way. They equip them with round shields woven from willow saplings and weighing twice as much as those used on the battlefield. They also give them wooden swords double the weight of real ones. So they are able to defend themselves better and to attack more vigorously. They are made to exercise in the afternoons as well as in the mornings, using this equipment against a wooden post. This is an invention which gives valuable training to gladiators as well as to soldiers. No man has ever distinguished himself either in the arena or on the battlefield without first going through a rigorous training at the post.

This is what the recruit does. He fixes a post about six feet in height firmly in the ground. He then practises fighting against the post, as if he is fighting an enemy. He uses his woven shield and wooden sword, as if he is using real ones. First, he attacks his opponent's head and face, then he goes for his sides and sometimes he attempts to hack at his thighs or legs. He steps back or thrusts forward this way and that as if fighting a real opponent, using every manoeuvre possible. Most important of all the training he receives is that he learns never to expose any part of his body to his opponent while aiming his own blows at him.

They are also taught not to cut with their swords but to thrust. The Romans find it so easy to beat people who use their swords to cut rather than thrust that they laugh in their faces. For a cutting stroke, even when made with full force, rarely kills. The vital organs are protected by the armour as well as by the bones of the body. On the other hand, a stab even two inches deep is usually fatal. So you have to make sure that whatever you cut the body with goes in far enough to reach the vital organs. Besides, if you attempt to cut rather than thrust with your sword, you expose your right arm and side. Yet when you deliver a thrust the body is protected and the enemy is wounded before he even sees the sword. This is the method of fighting that the Romans chiefly use.

Vegetius

1.2 The marching camp

If we look at the way the Romans organise their army, it soon becomes clear that this great empire of theirs came to them as a reward for their great skill, not as a gift of fortune.

The Romans do not sit about waiting for war to break out and then start training men to fight. They do not sit with their arms folded during peace time, waiting until there is a crisis, before getting to work. It is quite the opposite; it is as though they had been born with weapons in their hands. They never stop training, and they never wait for an emergency to arise. What is more, their exercises carried out in peace time are just as hard-fought as the real thing. Every soldier puts all he has into his training, just as if he were taking part in a real war. That is why they find it very easy

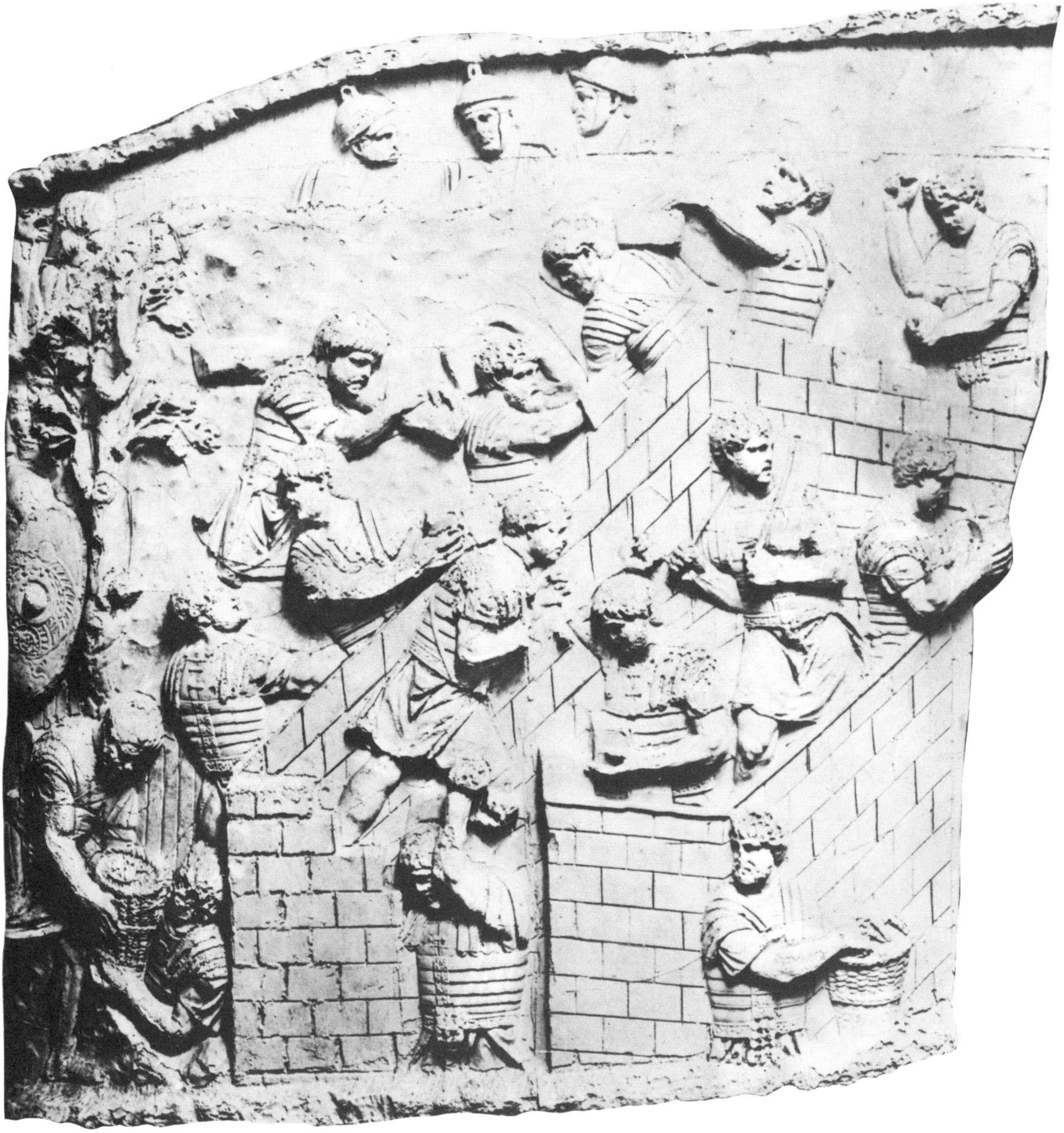

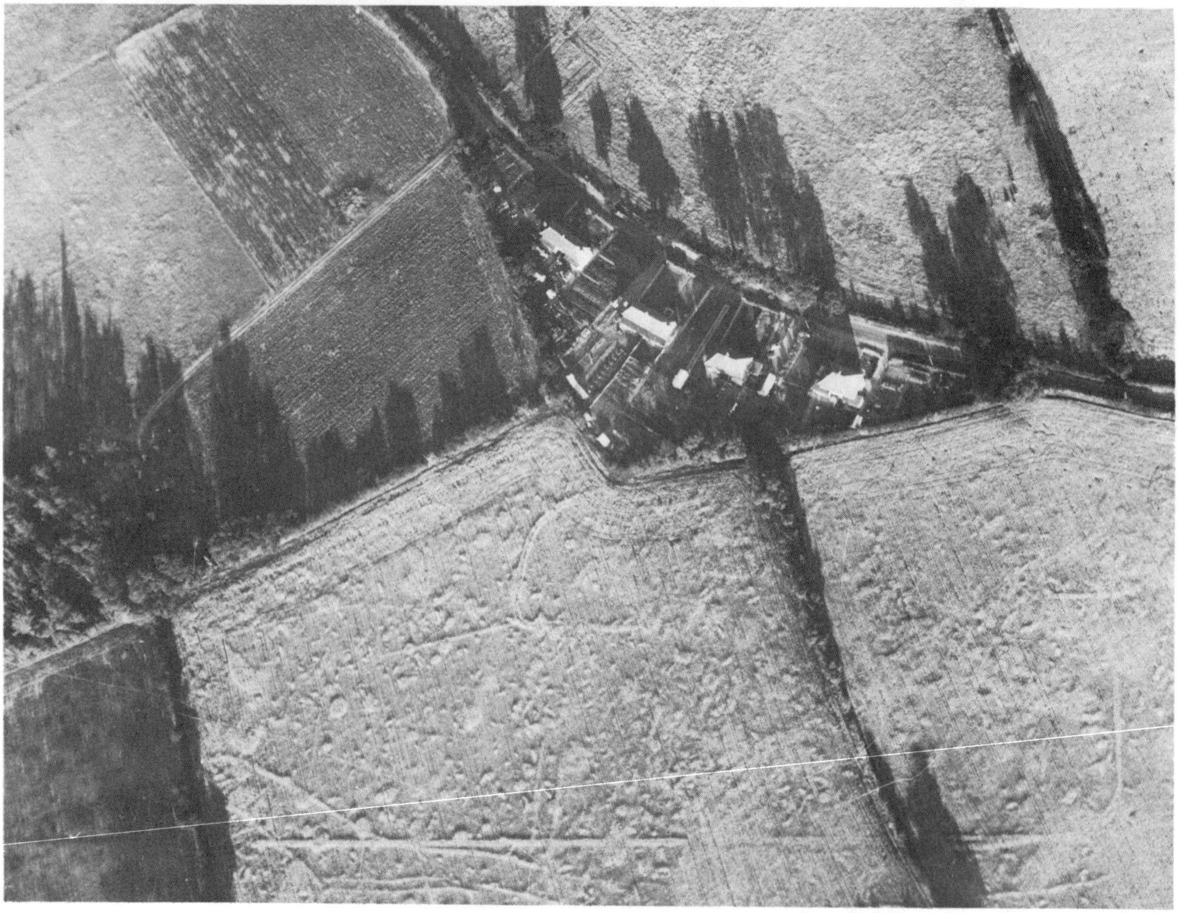

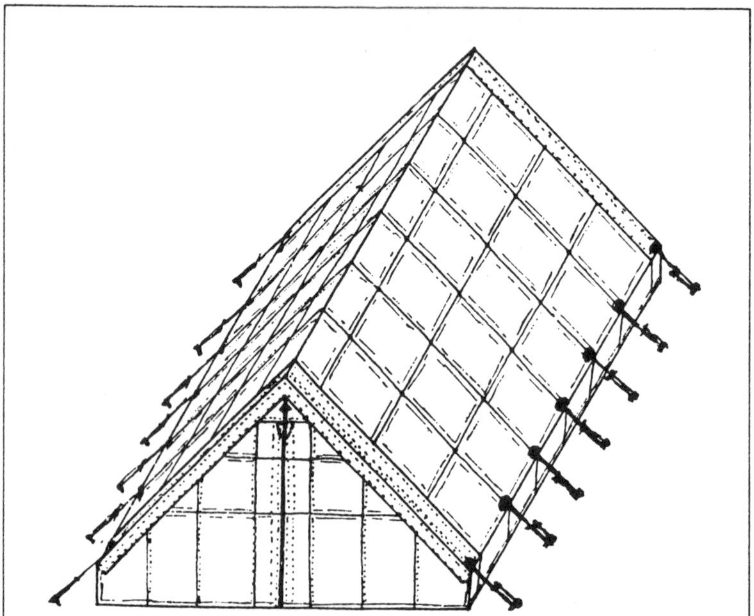

to fight battles with an enemy. And that is why their battle formation always holds together; they are never paralysed by fear or worn out with exhaustion. Their enemies are never a match for the Romans and so the Romans inevitably win. In fact, it would be true to say that their exercises are bloodless battles and their battles are bloody exercises.

The Romans never expose themselves to surprise attack. Whatever enemy country they may invade, they do not become involved in any battle before they have fortified their camp. They do not build it carelessly or on uneven ground. Nor do they set to work all at once or in a disorganised way. If the ground is uneven, they first level it off. Then they measure out a site for the camp in the form of a square. Attached to the army is a large number of workmen and they are equipped with tools for building.

The inside of the camp is divided up into rows of tents. The outer defences are made to look just like a wall and are equipped with towers at regular intervals. In the spaces between the towers, quick-firers, *ballistae*, onagers and every kind of artillery are placed ready for use. In this outer wall are set four gateways, one on each side. These are wide enough for the pack-animals to pass through without much difficulty and for troops to pour out of in case of emergency. The camp is crossed by streets laid out in an orderly plan. In the middle are the tents of the officers and at the very centre the legate has his headquarters, which look like a small temple. In this way a kind of city springs up, with its market square, places for the workers to live and its own law court, where the officers can pass judgement on any differences that arise between the men. The outer wall and all the buildings inside are constructed in no time at all, as there are so many skilled workmen to do the job. Just in case it should be necessary, the camp is also surrounded by a ditch, four cubits deep and four cubits wide.

Josephus *The Jewish War*

Notes 26 onager: a war machine for throwing large stones
38 four cubits: approximately 200 cm

The camp prefect

The camp prefect has many important responsibilities. He must choose a site for a camp and mark out the wall and ditch. He must organise the tents or soldiers' barracks along with their baggage. He is also responsible for seeing that medical treatment is available for sick soldiers. He must also see that the following items are always available: waggons, mules, saws, axes, spades, chisels, wood, straw, battering rams, onagers, *ballistae*, and every other type of siege machinery.

As the most knowledgeable man, he is chosen for the job after many years' outstanding service. He can then teach others what he has done well himself.

Vegetius

1.3 The army camp

This plan is based on a fortress at Inchtuthill in Scotland. The building was never completed. Fortresses were usually laid out in roughly the same way. Auxiliary forts were about one tenth of the size, but followed a similar plan (see Resource 2.6).

Key:
A Headquarters building
B Tribunes' house
C Drill hall
D Workshop
E Hospital
F Granaries
G Store rooms arranged in rows
H Barrack blocks. Each block holds one century. Eight men share a pair of rooms. The centurion has a suite of rooms at the end of the block.

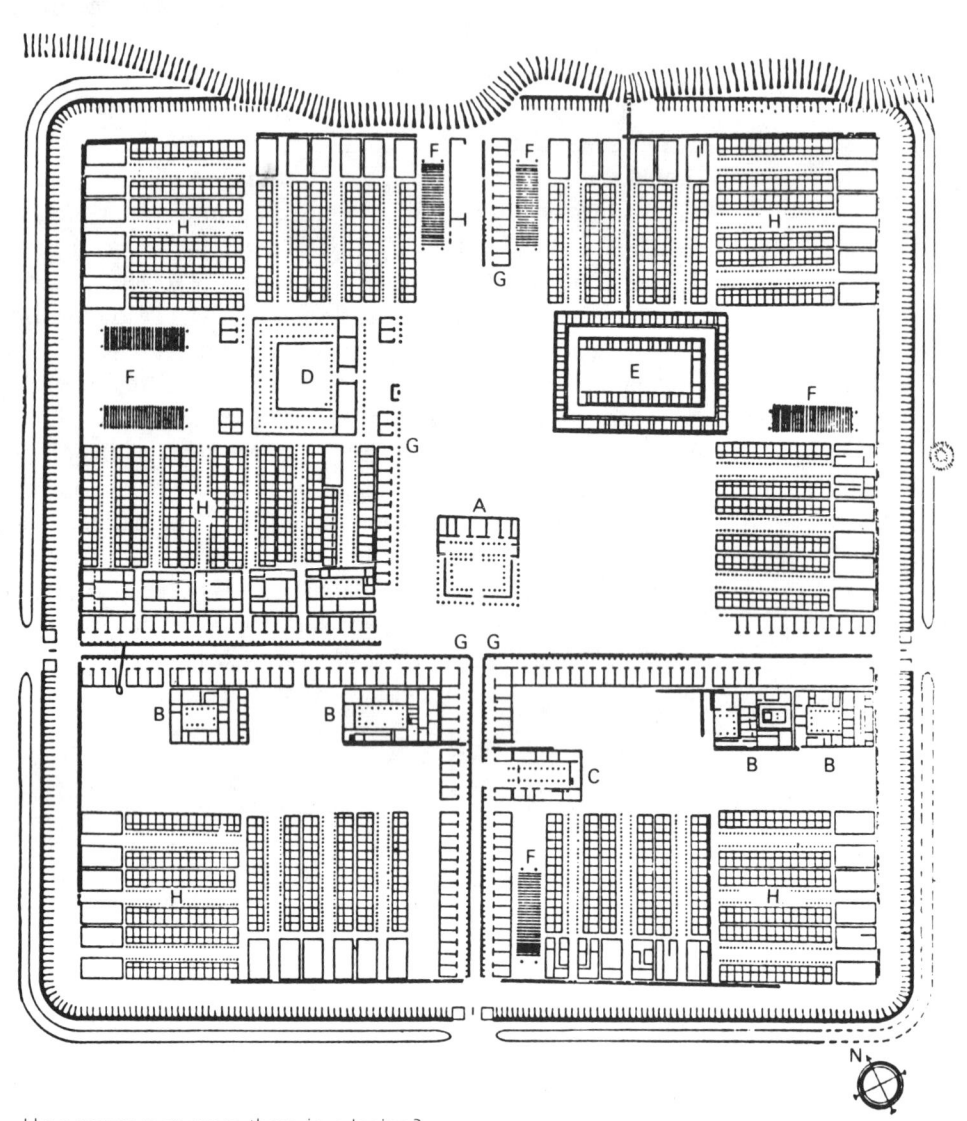

How many men were there in a legion?
1 century = 80 men commanded by a centurion
1 cohort = 6 centuries or 480 men
1 legion = 10 cohorts (one of these was double in size)
         = 5000+ commanded by a legate

Once they are encamped, the soldiers take up their quarters in tents, unit by unit. They do this quietly and in an orderly manner. They carry out all their other duties in the same way with the same discipline and attention to safety. This also applies when they go to collect wood, food supplies and the water they need. These jobs are shared out among the men. They do not have their supper or breakfast at any time they fancy, but they all eat at the same time. The time for going to bed, for beginning guard duty and for getting up are all announced by the sound of a trumpet, and nothing is done without a word of command. At dawn the ordinary soldiers report to their centurions. The centurions then go to salute the tribunes. The tribunes with the other officers then go to the legate for the morning salutation. The legate gives the officers the watchword and other orders which are to be passed on to the lower ranks. They act in the same organised way on the battlefield; whether they are on the attack or in retreat, the troops wheel round sharply in formation in the direction required as soon as the order is given.

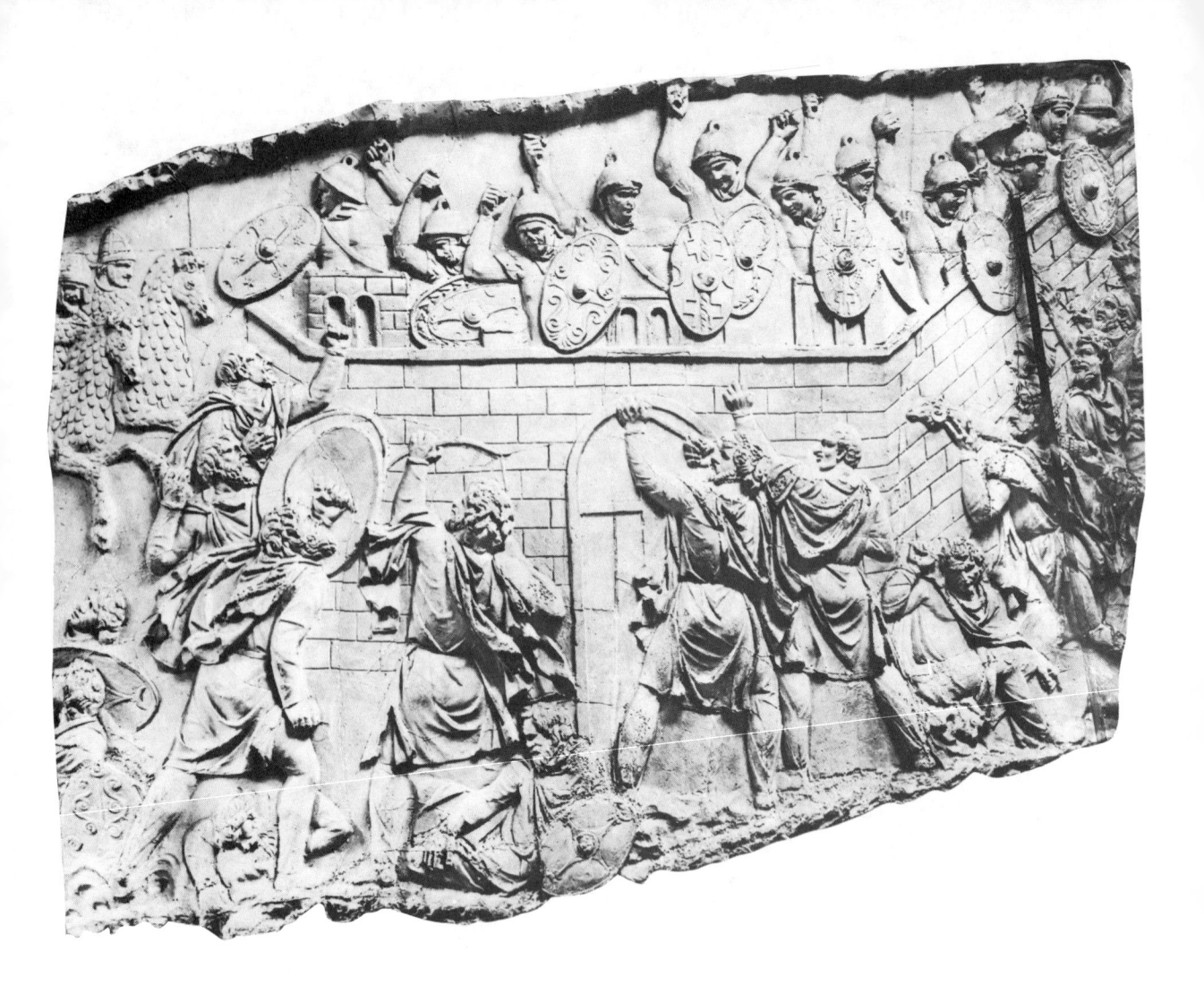

When they are ready to leave the camp, the trumpet sounds and
everyone jumps to it. Immediately, at this signal, they take down their
tents and get everything ready for the journey. A second trumpet call tells
them to prepare to march. Immediately, they pile up their baggage on the
mules and other pack-animals and stand there ready to set off, like runners
poised at the starting-line ready for a race. Then they set light to the camp,
for they always construct a new one at the point they have reached without
any difficulty and it is important to stop the enemy from ever making use
of it. For a third time the trumpets give the signal for departure. This is to
hurry up the stragglers, whatever the reason for the delay, and to make
sure that no one is missing from his place. Then the herald standing on the

right of the legate asks the troops in their native language whether they are
ready for war. Three times they shout out loudly and enthusiastically, 'Yes,
we are ready.' Some even reply before the words are out of the herald's
mouth. Then in a kind of warlike frenzy, they raise their right arms in the
air and give a shout. They march forward in silence and in good order with
each man keeping his place in the ranks as if they were face to face with
the enemy.

                                                                   Josephus   *The Jewish War*

A legion has builders, carpenters, masons, blacksmiths, painters and all the
rest of the craftsmen who are needed to build the winter quarters, to make
equipment, towers, fences and siege machinery, and who build and repair
weapons, waggons, and all kinds of artillery. There are workshops for
shields, breast-plates and bows, where they also make arrows, missiles,
helmets and all other types of armour. They are very concerned that
whatever the army needs should always be available in the camp.

                                                                           Vegetius

1.4 Roman soldiers on the march

The men move forward all marching in silence and in good order. Each
man keeps to his own position as if he were fighting.

  Foot-soldiers are armed with a cuirass and a helmet. They carry two
swords, one on each side. The one on the left is much longer than the
other. The one on the right is not much more than a span in length. The
soldiers chosen to form the general's bodyguard carry a spear and a round
shield. The ordinary soldier carries a javelin and a tall oblong shield. In
addition, he carries a saw, a basket, a mattock and an axe, as well as a
leather strap, a sickle, a chain, and enough rations to last him for three
days. In fact he carries so much equipment that he is not very different
from a pack-mule.

  Cavalrymen wear a long sword on the right and hold a long thrusting
spear in the hand. They have a large shield which rests on the horse's back
and a quiver with three or more weapons for throwing, which have broad
points and are as long as spears. Their helmets and cuirasses are the same
as those worn by all the foot-soldiers. The cavalrymen who have been
chosen to form the general's bodyguard are armed in exactly the same way
as the rest of the cavalry.

  The legion which is to lead the marching column is always chosen by
lot.

                                                              Josephus   *The Jewish War*

Note 5 a span: 22.5 cm

1.5 Testudo

This is how they make the formation which they call the *testudo*. The heavy-armed troops form a square with the baggage animals, the light-armed troops and the cavalry in the centre. The heavy-armed troops face outwards with their shields and weapons in the ready position. The others, densely packed in the square, raise their shields to cover their heads and interlock them. Nothing can be seen now except shields and all the men are protected against missiles. This roof of shields is so amazingly strong that men can walk on it, indeed even horses and chariots can be driven over it. The testudo is useful when they come to narrow passes. It is used in attacking forts for it enables the men to reach right up to the walls. Often when they are surrounded by archers they all crouch down together under their shields – even the horses are taught to kneel or lie down! This makes the enemy think that they are exhausted, but when the enemy comes near they spring up and surprise them.

Adapted from Dio Cassius

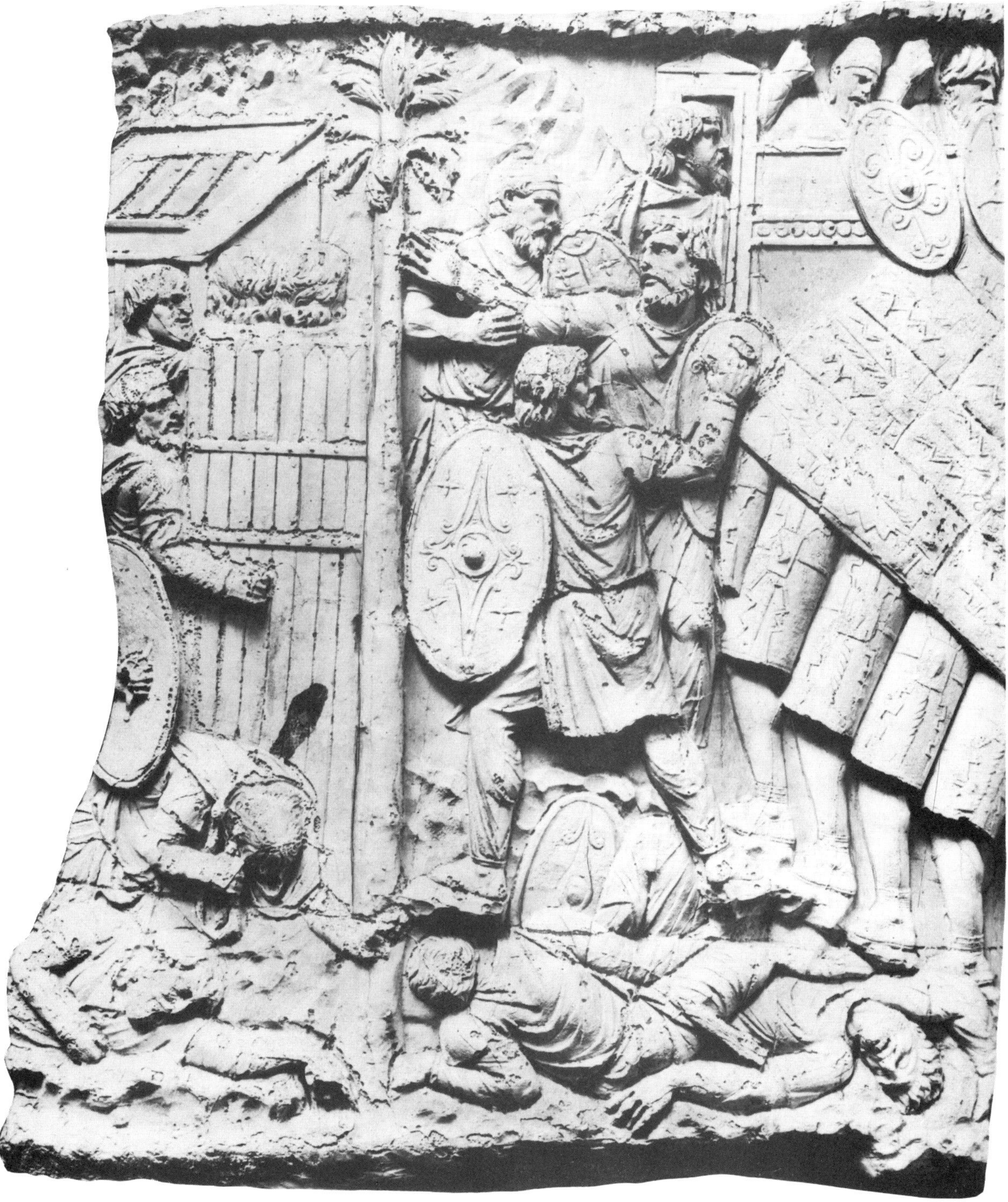

1.6 Treating the sick

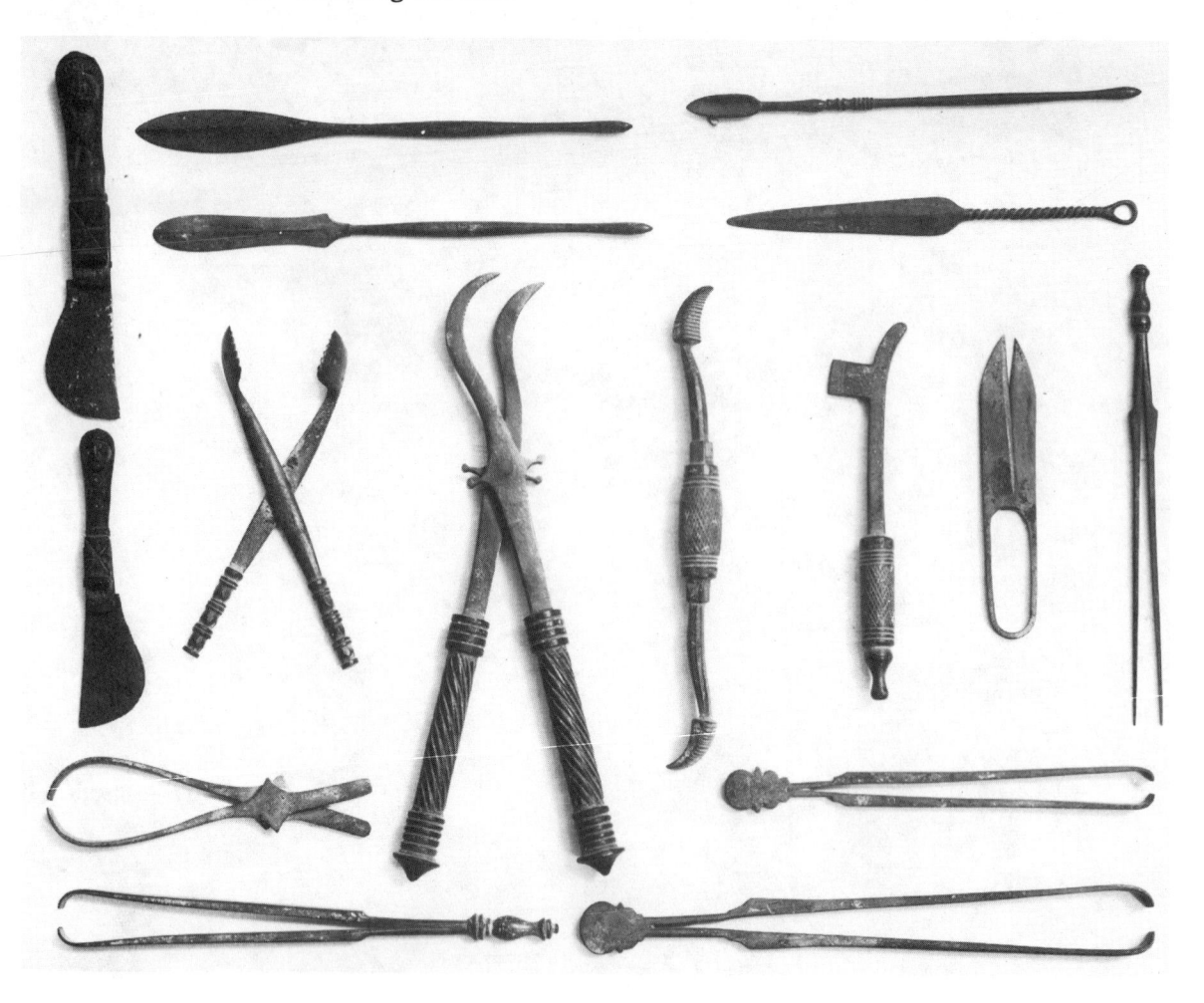

A Roman surgeon

A surgeon should be young or at least he should be youngish. He should have a strong and steady hand which never shakes and he should be ready to use his left hand as well as his right. His eyesight should be sharp and clear and he should have courage. He should feel sorry enough for the patient to want to cure him, but he should not be driven by his cries into working too fast or into cutting out less than is necessary. Instead he should carry on as if the cries of pain did not bother him at all.

Amputation of arms and legs

Sometimes gangrene develops between the fingernails or the toenails or under the armpits or in the groin. If the usual treatment fails to cure it, the arm or leg has to be amputated. But even this is a risky business, for patients often die during the operation either from loss of blood or from heart failure. However, it does not matter whether the remedy is safe

enough, as it is the only one. So between the good and bad parts, cut
through the flesh with a scalpel down as far as the bone. But you must
make sure that you don't cut over a joint. It is also better to cut off more
of the good part than you need rather than risk leaving any of the bad flesh
behind. When you get to the bone, you must pull back the flesh from the
bone and undercut all around it to make sure that some of the bone is
exposed. You must then cut through the bone with a small saw as near as
you can to the good flesh which still joins onto it. You must next smooth
down the end of the bone which has been roughened by the saw and pull
the skin back over it. You must make sure that the skin is sufficiently
loosened in the operation so that it covers the bone as far as possible. The
part where the skin does not reach must be covered with lint. Then a
sponge soaked in vinegar must be bandaged onto it.

Celsus

A doctor

... Gaius Stertinius Xenophon, son of Heraclitus of the Cornelian tribe, chief doctor of the divine emperors and secretary in charge of Greek affairs, military tribune, and *praefectus fabrum,* honoured at the British triumph with a gold crown and a spear ...

Inscription from the island of Cos

Note 32 *praefectus fabrum:* chief engineer

1.7 Armed forces in the Roman empire

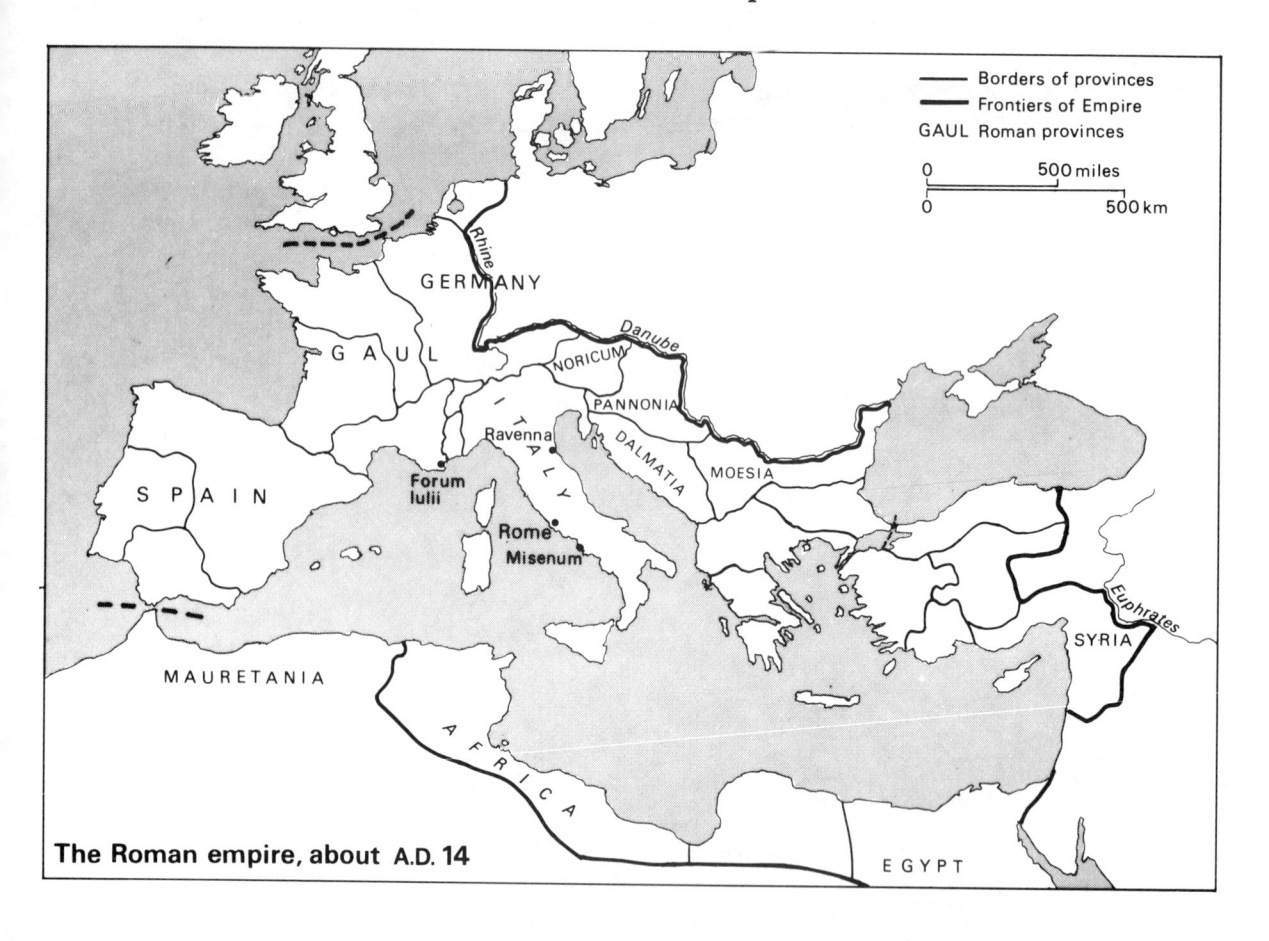

The Roman empire, about A.D. 14

The navy in A.D. 23

In Italy, on each coast there was a fleet, at Misenum and Ravenna. The southern coast of Gaul was protected by the warships which Augustus had captured in the battle of Actium and then sent fully manned to the town of Forum Iulii.

The army in A.D. 23

The greatest force was on the Rhine. Here there were eight legions and these served to protect both Gaul and Germany.

Spain, recently pacified, was held by three legions.

Mauretania had been handed over to King Juba as a gift from the Roman people.

The rest of Africa had two legions. There were also two in Egypt. In all that great expanse of land from Syria to the Euphrates there were four legions.

On the frontiers neighbouring kings received substantial support from us to help them protect themselves against foreign empires.

On the Danube frontier there were two legions in Pannonia and two in

Moesia. There were also two in Dalmatia, posted well behind the frontier, and so not far from Italy. Hence, if there was an emergency they could be brought in without delay.

The city had its own troops – the three urban cohorts and the nine praetorian cohorts.

At suitable places in the provinces our allies supplied triremes, cavalry squadrons, and auxiliary cohorts. There were about as many auxiliaries as there were legionaries. But it is difficult to give precise details, as they were moved around according to need, and their numbers were continually changing.

Tacitus *Annals*

Note 21 The city: Rome

Legionaries air their grievances

In the confusion following the fall of Nero, Otho became emperor. There was unrest in the army.

The legionaries demanded that they should no longer have to bribe the centurions to secure exemption from duties. For the ordinary legionary this amounted to an annual tax. As long as the centurion received his money a quarter of the men could be off on leave, or just lounging around in the camp. No one cared how the soldiers got the money for the tax or the difficulties this caused. In fact they got the money to buy themselves off duties by highway robbery, thieving and doing menial jobs. Moreover the richest soldiers had to suffer the centurion's cruelty. They were assigned all the worst duties until they bought themselves relief. When his money was gone and his energy exhausted, the legionary came back poor instead of rich, lazy instead of eager. So man after man was ruined by the same poverty and poor discipline; then they were very keen to get involved in rebellions, riots and even civil war.

However, the emperor did not want, by his generosity to the legionaries, to cause trouble among the centurions. Instead he promised to pay for annual exemptions from the Imperial Treasury. This measure was certainly useful, and good rulers afterwards made this one of the principles of service.

Tacitus *Histories*

1.8 A papyrus from Egypt

Many letters have survived in the sands of Egypt written on papyrus. Among them is this letter from a soldier serving in the Roman army.

Theonas to Tetheus, his lady mother, many greetings.

I wanted you to know that the reason I have taken so long to send you a letter is that I am in camp–and not because I am ill; so do not get upset. I was upset to hear that you had heard bad news of me, for I was not seriously ill. It's the fault of the person who told you. Do not bother to send me anything. I received the presents from Heraclides. Dionytas my brother, brought me the present and I received your letter. I always give thanks to the gods . . . all the time . . .

Do not go to the trouble of sending me anything . . .

1.9 The emperor triumphs

Before setting out for war a Roman general would visit the temple of Jupiter Best and Greatest on the Capitol. There he would ask the gods' help, promising gifts if the war was successful. The usual gift offered was the spray of laurel which the victorious general had entwined round his *fasces*. But in special circumstances and after a great victory the general would ask the senate for permission to hold a triumph.

It was not lawful for a general to enter the city with his army except to celebrate a triumph so the troops waited in a camp on the Field of Mars until permission came. Then they formed up in a great procession and entered the cheering city through the Triumph gate.

First came the blaring of the trumpeters, then the *popae* carrying their axes and mallets while their assistants drove a herd of milk-white oxen whose horns were painted gold and hung with ribbons of bright wool and chains of flowers. These oxen were for sacrifice. Beside them walked the long-haired boys *(camilli)*, the sons of noble families. They carried incense boxes, pitchers of wine and plates of salted meal – all needed for the sacrifice. Now came the soldiers with plumes fixed on their helmets and armour glittering, and the standard-bearers in their animal skins holding up the victorious eagles and the banners of the cohorts; and on poles men carried the golden crowns presented to their general by each of the cities he had passed through on his way home from the battlefield.

Men bent under the weight of the wooden platforms they carried on their shoulders piled high with booty – rich treasures of gold and silver and precious stones and the armour of the enemy. They dragged carts on which tottered great statues of the defeated generals and their defeated gods; they pulled floats on which were built replicas of conquered cities, rivers, castles, mountains, lakes and seas and re-enactments of their battles.

Conquered kings and queens and their children walked in chains beside the chariots. All the time the soldiers sang rude and indecent songs about their general or chanted again and again 'Io triumphe! Io triumphe!'

Last of all came the triumphant general sitting in a chariot drawn by four horses. His tunic was embroidered with palm leaves and his toga was woven with purple and gold. In his hand he held a branch of laurel. Behind him in the chariot stood a slave holding a crown above his master's head and whispering in his ear, 'Remember that thou art mortal! Look behind! Look behind!'

A bell and a whip were fastened to the chariot to remind the general that is was still possible for him to fall into misery again, even to be condemned to scourging or to death.

The procession wound its way through cheering crowds past the Circus Maximus, round the Palatine Hill, then along the Via Sacra through the Forum, past the Rostra, then up the Capitoline Hill to the temple of Jupiter Capitolinus. There at last the general offered up his sacrifice and gifts in thanksgiving to the god. And then he went home in the evening to the sound of pipes.

The days or even weeks which followed would be filled with games and entertainments for the people – all paid for by the general out of his loot.

Compiled from various sources

Notes 5 *fasces*: staff of office carried in front of the most important Roman magistrates
11 *popae*: priest's assistants who slaughtered sacrificial animals

Evidence for Claudius' triumphal arch

'To the emperor Tiberius Claudius, son of Drusus, Caesar Augustus Germanicus, Pontifex Maximus, holding tribunician power for the eleventh time, Consul for the fifth time, saluted as *Imperator* twenty-two times, Censor, Father of his Country. This was set up by the senate and people of Rome, because he received the formal surrender of eleven British kings, who were defeated without any loss and because he was the first to bring barbarian peoples on the other side of Oceanus under Roman rule.'

Resources 2 More about the Britons

2.1 Evidence from southern Britain

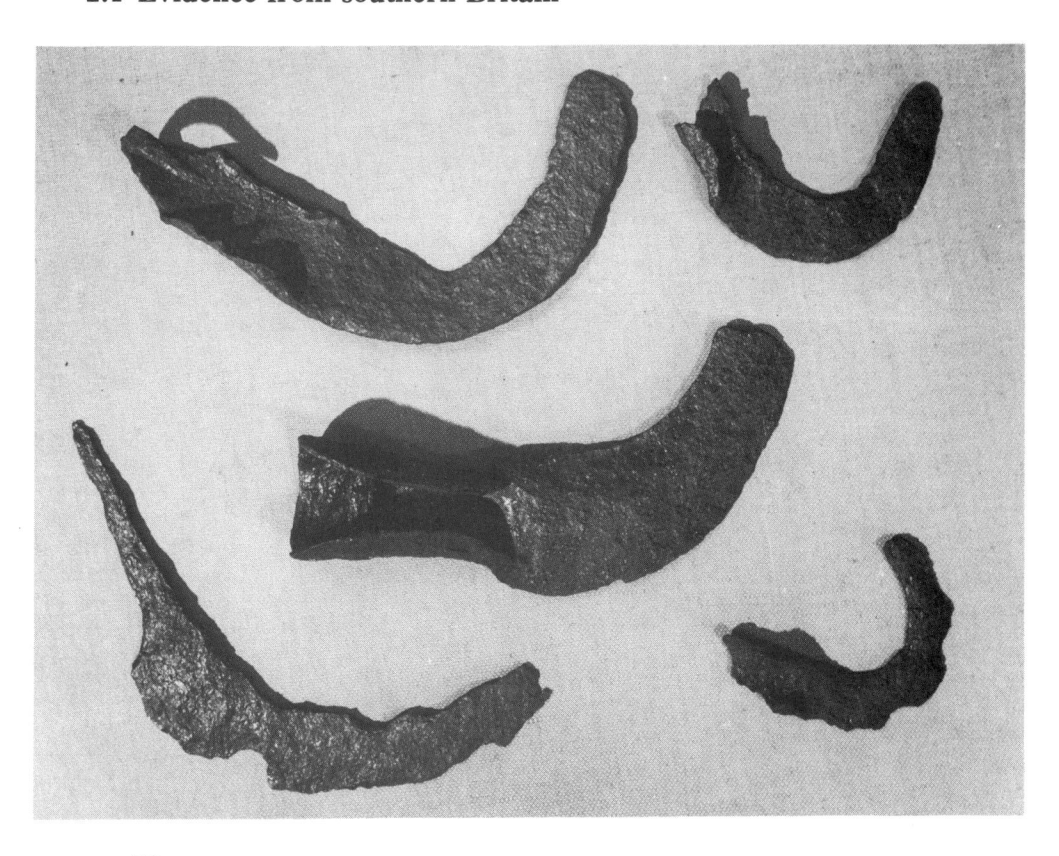

54

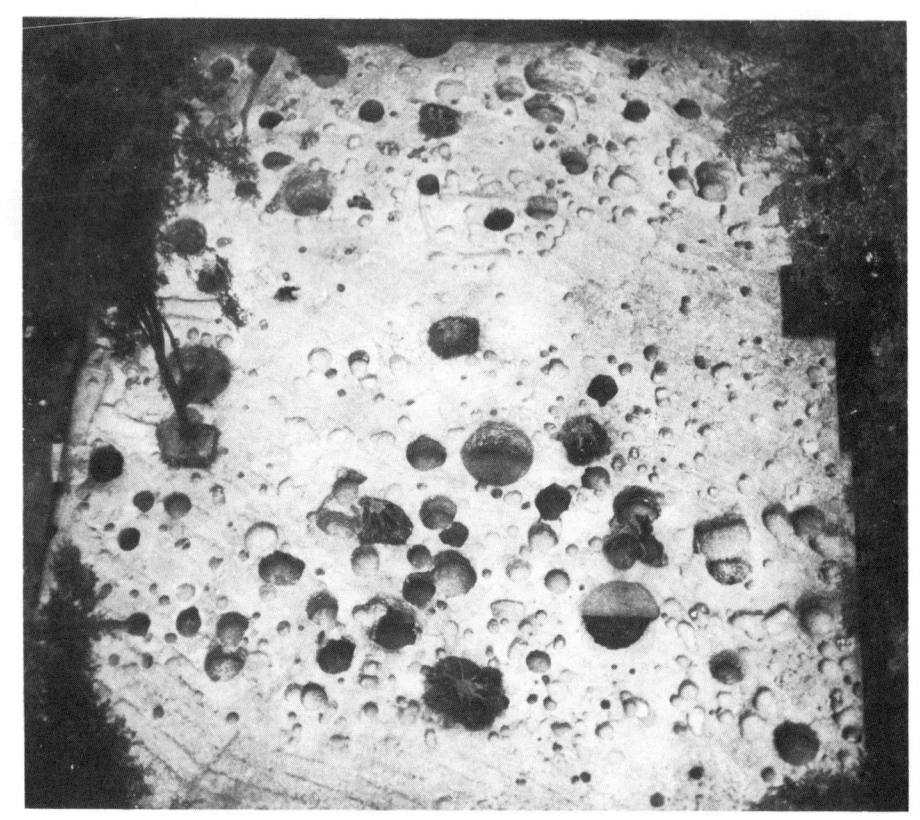

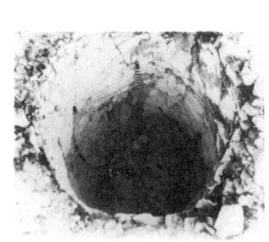

2.2 Evidence from northern Britain

A very large quantity of animal bones was excavated from Stanwick, an iron age site with substantial earthworks in North Yorkshire. The following table gives approximate percentages of animal bones found:

ox	40%
sheep	23%
pig	16%
horse	13%
dog	4%
roe deer	1%
red deer	1%
hare	1%

2.3 British hill forts

2.4 A British burial

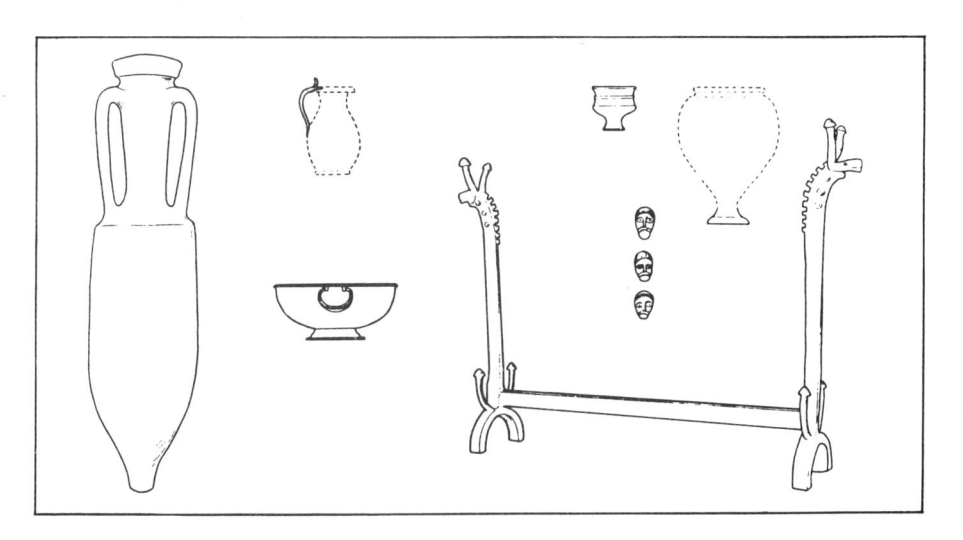

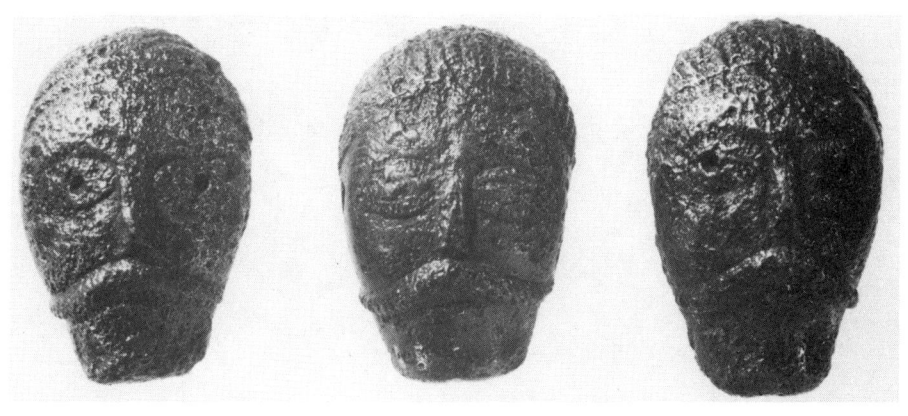

2.5 Found at a British settlement

2.6 The search for metals

British tin

The inhabitants of Britain who live round the promontory known as
Belerion are very hospitable to strangers and have become civilised because
of their contact with traders and other people. These people work the tin,
treating the ground which contains it in a clever way. The ground is like
rock but it has earthy seams in it from which the tin workers quarry the
ore. This they then melt down to remove the impurities. They then work
the tin into pieces the size of knuckle-bones and transport it to an island
which lies off the cost of Britain called Ictis. When the tide goes out they
are able to take large amounts of tin over to the island on their
waggons ... On the island of Ictis, traders buy the tin from the natives and
carry it from there across the water to Gaul. They make their journey on
foot through Gaul for about thirty days and arrive with their wares on
horseback at the mouth of the River Rhône.

Diodorus of Sicily

Notes 3 Belerion: Cornwall
9 Ictis: probably St Michael's Mount

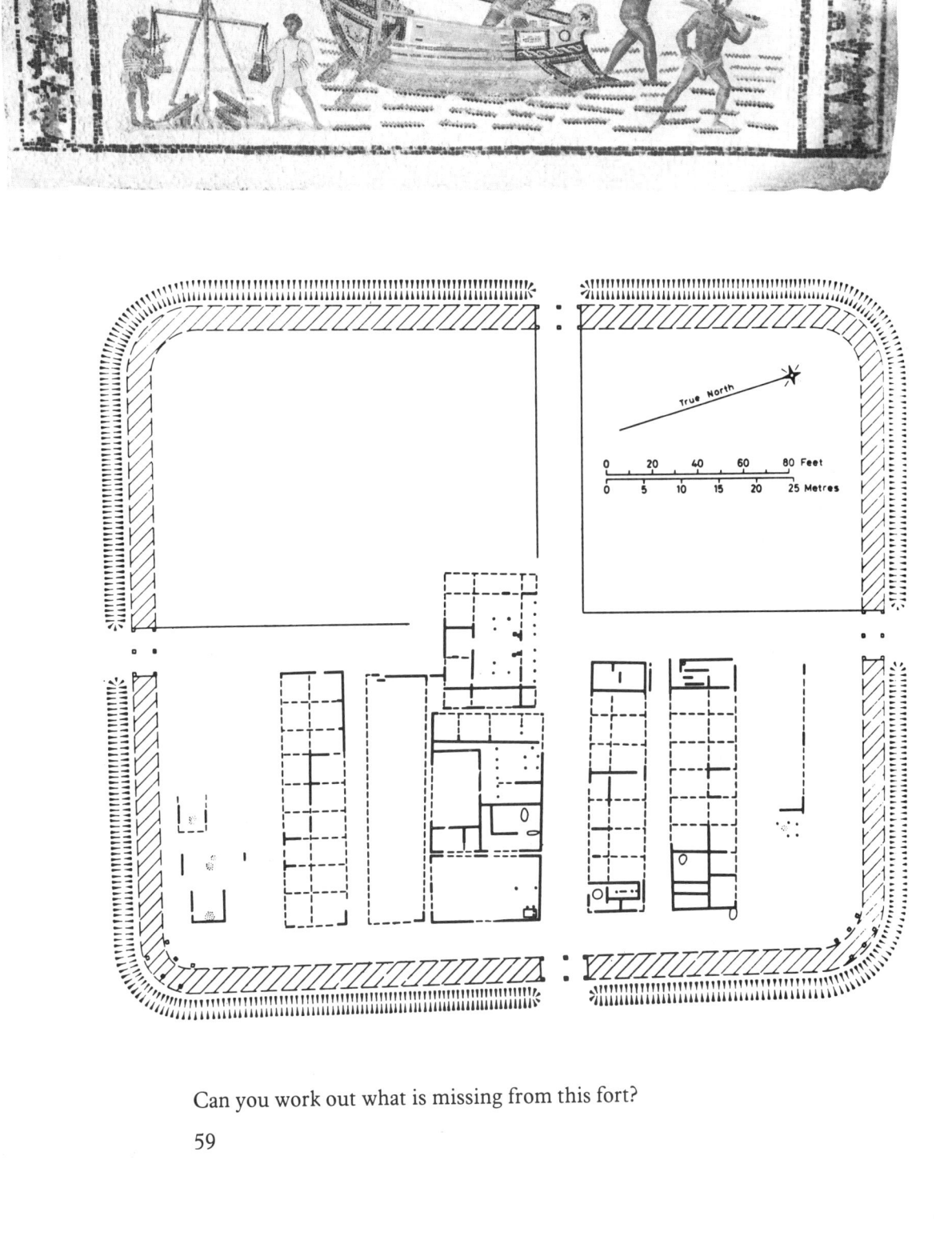

Can you work out what is missing from this fort?

2.7 Maiden Castle

Is this one of the *oppida* mentioned by Suetonius? (see p.22) **(Clue 8)**

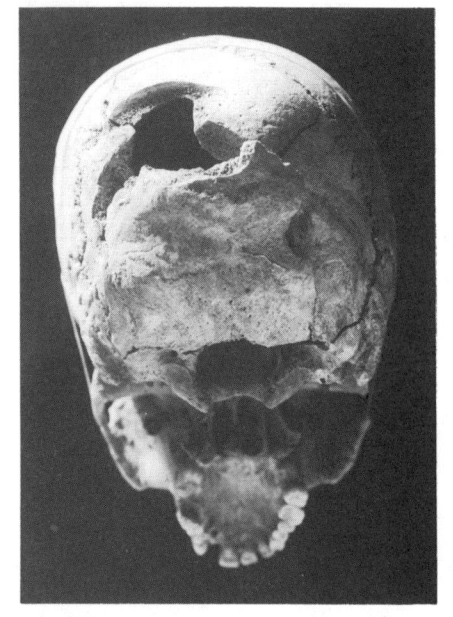

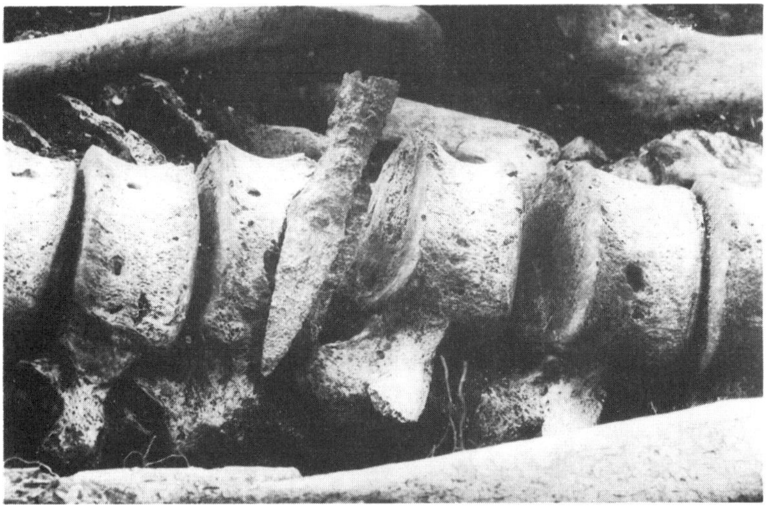

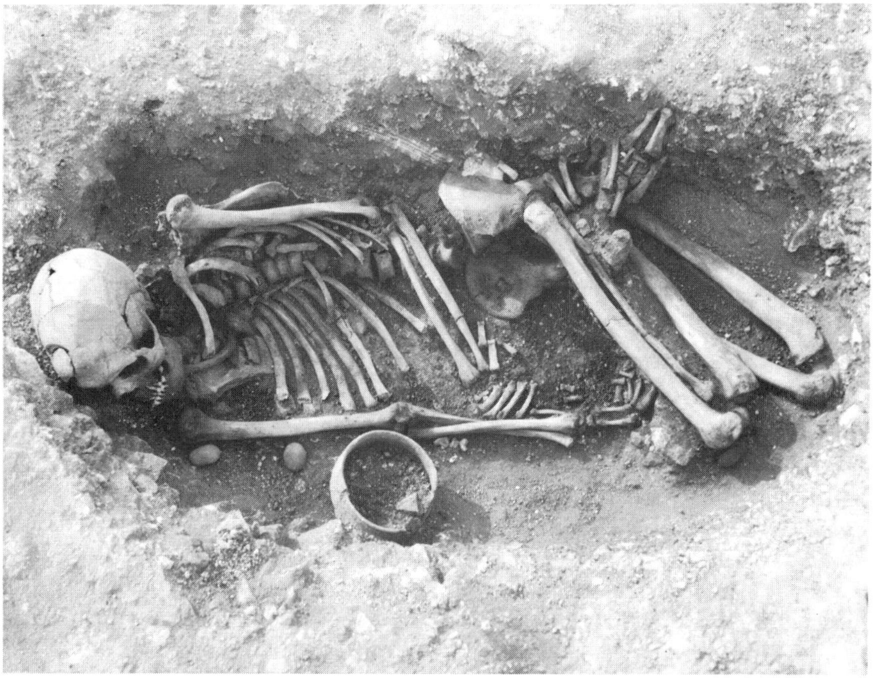

2.8 Cogidubnus, the tribal king

Was the palace at Fishbourne built for him? **(Clue 9)**

To Neptune and Minerva, for the health and safety of the divine house by the authority of Tiberius Claudius Cogidubnus, Great King in Britain. The society of smiths and its members gave this temple out of their own funds.
　. . . ens, the son of Pudentinus, gave the land to build on.

Inscription from Chichester

Roman palace
Roman road

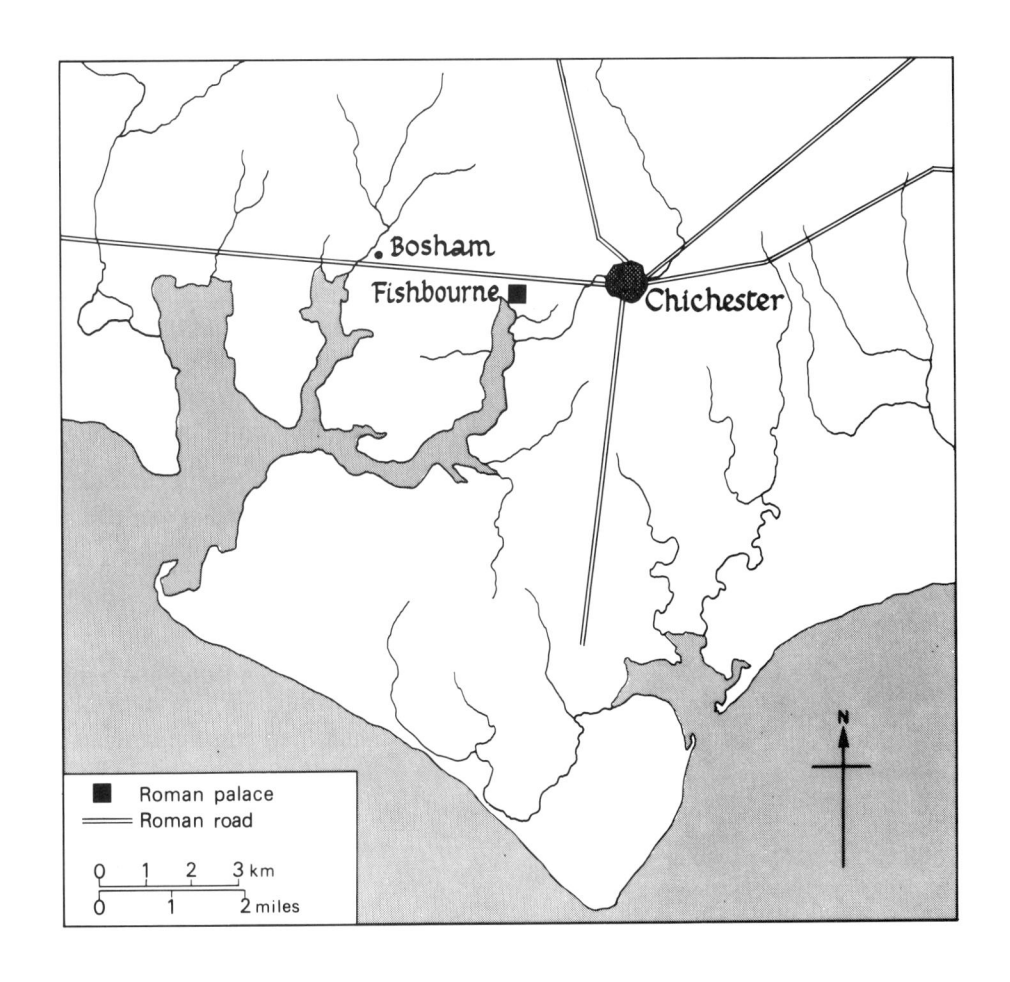

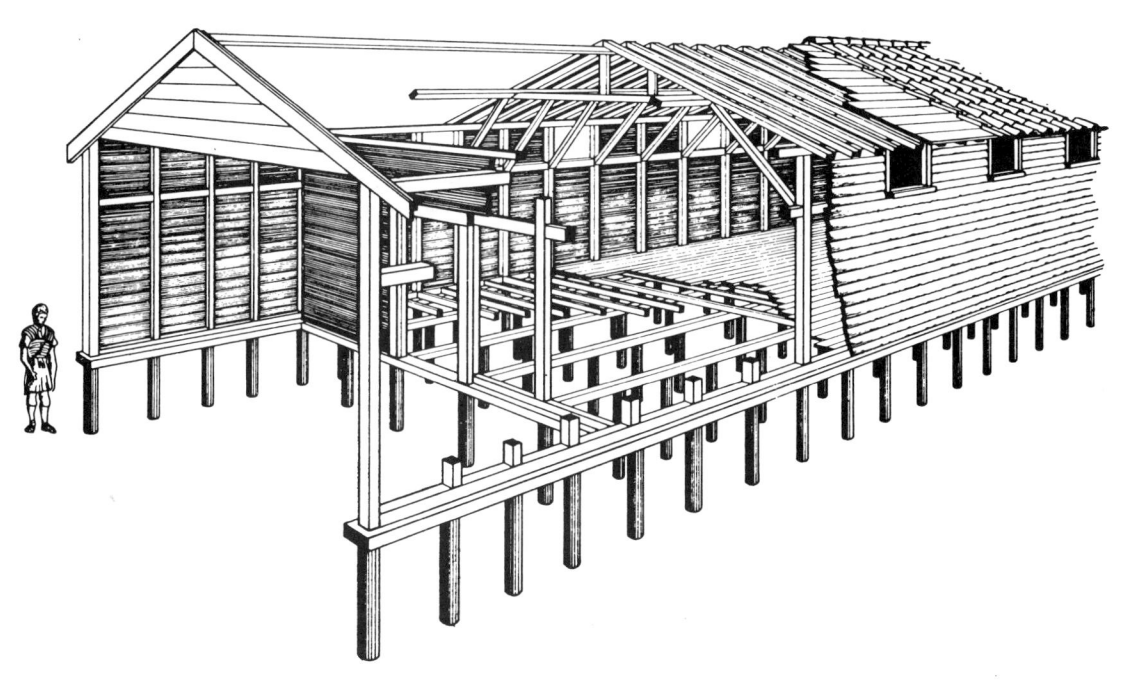

Resources 3 Making sense of Roman inscriptions

Inscriptions are sometimes dug up by archaeologists, sometimes discovered by chance. They often contain important evidence about the Romans in Britain. Here is a translation of an inscription found at Wroxeter:

'Titus Flaminius, son of Titus, of the Pollian voting-tribe, from Faventia, aged 45, of 22 years' service, a soldier of the Fourteenth Legion Gemina. I did my service and now I am here. Read this, whether you are more or less lucky than I. The gods do not allow you the wine-grape and water once you have entered the Underworld. Live a good life while your star allows you to be alive.'

What kind of inscription is this? How can you tell? Make a list of all the information that we can learn about Flaminius from this inscription. What else can we infer from this tombstone?

Deciphering the code

The following inscriptions are all in their original language of Latin, and reproduced in the exact form in which they were inscribed by the stonemason. Many of the words are shortened and the language is difficult to decipher.

What sort of information would we normally expect to find on inscriptions? (Refer back to Flaminius' inscription.)

On the inscriptions that follow can you work out:

1 **Names:** Roman citizens had three names.

The first name is usually shortened: Sex.Sextus; C.Gaius; M.Marcus; Cn.Gnaeus; T.Titus.
The second name (of a man) usually ends in IVS.
All three names are not always given together; sometimes the voting-tribe (e.g. Gal(erian) or Pol(lian)) is put between the second and third names. Roman citizens, wherever they came from, had to be enrolled in one of the thirty-five Roman voting-tribes. By the time of Claudius, these seem to have been used only for registration purposes.

2 **Age at death:** AN(NORVM) (followed by the number)

3 **Years of service:** STIP(ENDIA) (followed by the number)

4 **Legion or cohort to which he belonged:** LEG(IO) (followed by the number) *or* if he was a cavalryman: EQ(V)ES (followed by his cohort)

What information can we work out from the following group of inscriptions as a whole?

Two of the inscriptions do not belong to soldiers. Can you identify them? What can you learn about these two people?

Here is some additional information which may be helpful.

M.F(ILIVS) = Son of Marcus. How many other inscriptions have 'son of'?

CIVIS = A citizen of (followed by name of his community)

BEN(EFICIARIVS) = An assistant to the governor

MIL(ES) = A soldier

SIGN(IFER)
AQVILIF(ER) } = A standard bearer

FRATER = Brother

H.S.E. = *(hic situs est)* Here (he) lies

D.M. = To the *Manes* of ... What words can you suggest to translate *Manes*?

HEREDES = Heirs

What other kinds of inscription can you find? Look first of all for examples in this book.

3.1 Tombstone of a cavalryman found at Gloucester (Clue 10)

3.2 Tombstone of a centurion found at Colchester (Clue 11)

3.3 Tombstone of a standard-bearer found in Germany

CN·MVSIVS·T·F
GAL·VELEIAS·AN·
XXXII·STIP·XV
AQVILIF·LEG·XIIII·GEM
M·MVSIVS·FRATER·POSVIT

3.4 Tombstones found at Cirencester

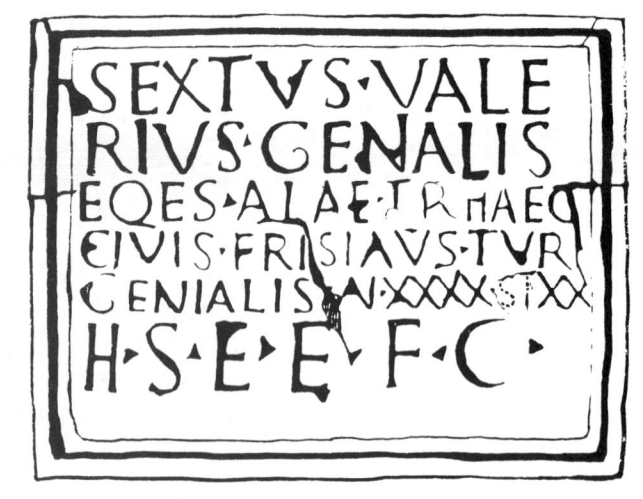

PHILVS·CA
SSAVI·FILI·
CIVIS·SEQV
ANN   XXXXV
H·S E

SEXTVS·VALE
RIVS·GENALIS
EQES·ALAE·T·RHAEC
CIVIS·FRISIAVS·TVR
GENIALIS·AN·XXXX·ST·XX
H·S·E·E·F·C·

3.5 Tombstones found at Wroxeter (Clue 12)

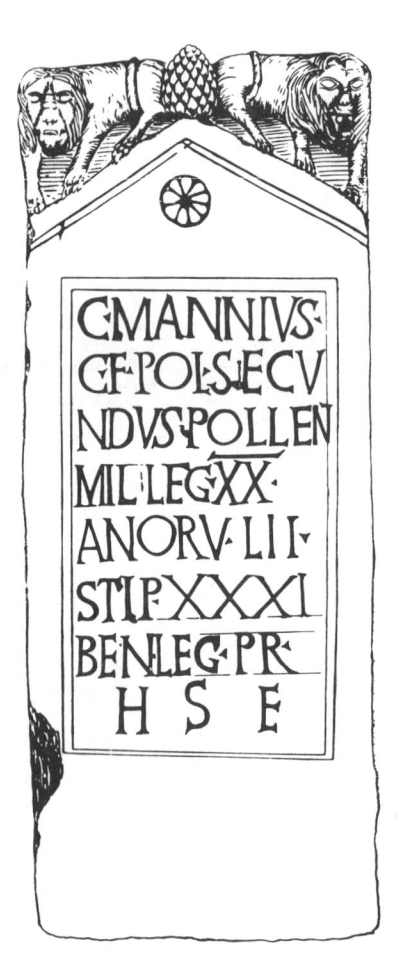

C·MANNIVS·
C·F·POL·SECV
NDVS·POLLEN
MIL·LEG·XX·
ANOR·V·LII·
STIP·XXXI
BEN·LEG·PR
H S E

M·PETRONIVS
L·F·MEN
VIC·ANN
XXXVIII
MIL·LEG
····GEM
MILITAVIT
ANN·XVIII
SIGN·F·VIT
H·S·E

3.6 Tombstones found at Lincoln (Clue 13)

```
D  D  M
CLAVDIAE
CRYSIDI
VIXIT
AN  LXXXX
HEREDES
P  C
```

```
C·SAVFEIO
C·F·FAB·HER
MILIT·LEGIO
VIII
ANNOR·XXXX
STIP·XXII
H·S·E
```

3.7 Tombstone found at Caerleon

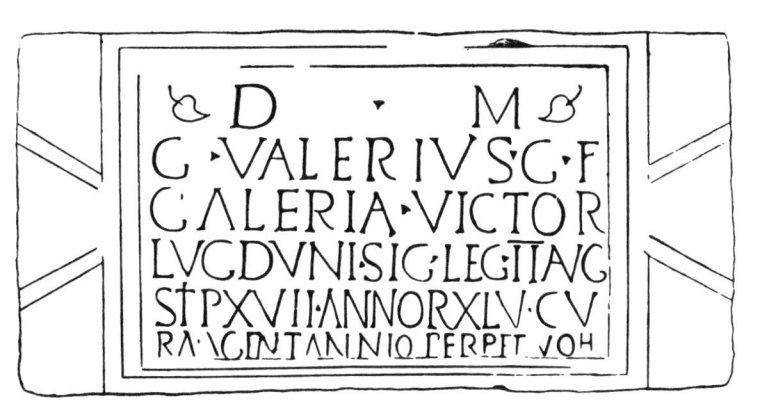

```
D  ·  M
C·VALERIVS·C·F
GALERIA·VICTOR
LVGDVNI·SIG·LEG·II·AVG
STP·XVII·ANNOR·XLV·CV
RA·C·IN·TANNIO·PERPIT·VOH
```

Greek and Roman writers

Aristotle (384–322 B.C.) was a famous Greek philosopher and scientist. He founded an important school in Athens, a forerunner of modern universities. He wrote many works but others were written by later writers in imitation of Aristotle. These writings are referred to as Pseudo-Aristotle.

Caesar Gaius Julius Caesar was born about 100 B.C. He showed a keen interest in politics at an early age. From 59–49 B.C. he was given the governorship of Gaul and Illyricum. He extended the Roman province of Gaul as far as the English Channel and twice (in 55 and 54 B.C.) made expeditions to Britain.

Caesar's policies and attitudes did not prove acceptable to the senators of Rome and he was assassinated in 44 B.C. He was well-known as a public speaker and lucid writer. His works include the seven books he wrote about his campaigns in Gaul.

Catullus Gaius Valerius Catullus (born about 84 B.C. and died about 54 B.C.) was a poet. He was born in northern Italy and came to live in Rome. Some of his most famous poems are those addressed to his mistress Lesbia.

Celsus Aulus Cornelius Celsus wrote an encyclopedia during the reign of Tiberius (A.D.14–37). Only the section on medicine has survived.

Cicero Marcus Tullius Cicero (106–43 B.C.) was a famous writer, orator and politician of his day. He was active in Roman politics at the same time as Julius Caesar. Cicero's writings which have survived include speeches, philosophy and a very large quantity of private letters.

Dio Cassius Cassius Dio Cocceianus (born in the second half of the 2nd century A.D.) was a Greek historian who came from Bithynia in Asia Minor. He wrote a history of Rome from its origins to A.D.229, which survives in part.

Diodorus Diodorus Siculus (of Sicily) lived at the time of Julius Caesar and Augustus. He was a Greek who wrote a history of the world from earliest times to Julius Caesar's conquest of Gaul.

Herodotus (5th century B.C.) came from Halicarnassus in Asia Minor. He is often called 'the father of history'. He wrote a history of the 5th century wars between the Greeks and the Persians. He travelled widely in the ancient world and his history includes a good deal of description of the geography of the ancient world and the peoples who inhabited it.

Homer	(8th century B.C.) the earliest and most famous Greek poet who is said to have written *The Iliad* and *The Odyssey*. He probably put together the poems in their final form using the descriptions and story material which he received from a long line of poets before his own day.
Horace	Quintus Horatius Flaccus (65 B.C. to about 8 B.C.) was the son of a freedman. From a humble beginning, he rose to the position of unofficial poet laureate to Augustus. Among his works were four books of odes.
Josephus	Flavius Josephus lived in the 1st century A.D. He was a Jewish priest and of noble birth. In the Jewish revolt of A.D.67, he was put in command of Galilee, but was captured by the legate Vespasian. Josephus saved his own life by prophesying that Vespasian would one day become emperor. Vespasian was emperor from A.D.69 to 79. Josephus was granted Roman citizenship and settled in Rome. He wrote an account of the Jewish war in Greek.
Plutarch	(born before A.D.50 and died after A.D.120) spent most of his life on the mainland of Greece and at Rome. He wrote many books including works of philosophy and a series of parallel biographies of famous Greeks and Romans.
Strabo	(born 64 or 63 B.C. and died after A.D.21) was a Greek writer of history and geography and came from Pontus in Asia Minor. He spent some time at Rome but it is unlikely that he ever visited Britain or Gaul.
Suetonius	Gaius Suetonius Tranquillus (born about A.D.70) spent most of his life in the imperial service. His main work is his *Lives of the Caesars*, biographies of Julius Caesar and the first eleven emperors from Augustus to Domitian. As secretary to the Emperor Hadrian, Suetonius had access to official records, but he also makes use of gossip and many other sources.
Tacitus	Cornelius Tacitus (about A.D.56 to the early 2nd century A.D.) was a skilled orator, who turned to writing history. His writings included a biography of his father-in-law, Agricola, who had been governor of Britain (A.D.78–84), and two major historical works *The Annals* and *The Histories*.
Vegetius	Flavius Vegetius Renatus is the latest of our writers. He wrote a military handbook at the end of the 4th century A.D. although much of his material refers to earlier times. He was neither a soldier nor an historian but an official in the imperial service.

Some Roman emperors

Augustus
27 B.C.–A.D. 14

Tiberius
14–37

Caligula
37–41

Claudius
41–54

Nero
54–68

Galba, Otho, Vitellius
68–69

Vespasian
69–79

Titus
79–81

Domitian
81–96

Nerva
96–8

Trajan
98–116

Hadrian
117–138

Antoninus Pius
138–161

Lucius Verus
161–169

Marcus Aurelius
161–180

Commodus
180–193